KR
PB LR

D0016775

MOURNERS

MOURNERS

A Nameless Detective Novel

Bill Pronzini

THORNDIKE
CHIVERS

This Large Print edition is published by Thorndike Press®, Waterville, Maine USA and by BBC Audiobooks Ltd, Bath, England.

Published in 2006 in the U.S. by arrangement with St. Martin's Press, LLC.

Published in 2006 in the U.K. by arrangement with the author.

U.S. Hardcover   0-7862-8575-3   (Mystery)
U.K. Hardcover 10: 1 4056 3771 4   (Chivers Large Print)
U.K. Hardcover 13: 978 1 405 63771 8
U.K. Softcover 10: 1 4056 3772 2   (Camden Large Print)
U.K. Softcover 13: 978 1 495 63772 5

The text of this Large Print edition is unabridged.
Other aspects of the book may vary from the original edition.

Set in 16 pt. Plantin by Christina S. Huff.

Printed in the United States on permanent paper.

British Library Cataloguing-in-Publication Data available

Library of Congress Cataloging-in-Publication Data

Pronzini, Bill.
    Mourners : a nameless detective novel / by Bill Pronzini.
        p. cm. — (Thorndike Press large print mystery)
    ISBN 0-7862-8575-3 (lg. print : hc : alk. paper)
        1. Nameless Detective (Fictitious character) — Fiction.
    2. Private investigators — California — San Francisco —
    Fiction.   3. San Francisco (Calif.) — Fiction.   4. Large
    type books.   I. Title.   II. Thorndike Press large print
    mystery series.
    PS3566.R67M68 2006b
        813′.6—dc22   2006004719

Acknowledgments

With thanks to the three M's — Marcia, Melissa Meith, Melissa Ward — and to Joe Chernicoff for their help and encouragement.

We must all come to terms. For we must all lie down in darkness. And when we do we take the measure of ourselves.

— H. R. Hays,
Lie Down in Darkness

1

It was a small, private funeral at the Glade Brothers Mortuary in Daly City. Different in all respects from the two funerals the day before. Both of those had been large affairs held in San Francisco, one in a funeral home in the Marina and the other at Mission Dolores.

The bereaved were still gathering when we got there. Half a dozen cars were parked in the adjacent lot, and there were little knots of ethnically mixed individuals outside the mortuary's entrance; the age and makes of the cars and the mourners' dark suits and dark dresses said they were a low-income group. Troxell went straight inside, as on the other occasions, without speaking or acknowledging anybody, but this time I didn't tag along to watch him view the remains and then sit like a rock in one of the pews throughout the service. I dislike funerals in principle; honoring the dead should be a personal and private act, not a ritualistic public spectacle. And I'd already exceeded my low tolerance level for dirge music, the sweet cloying scent of flowers, faces ravaged by pain and grief. I stayed in the car, wishing for maybe the twentieth time that Jake Runyon hadn't been too busy to pull this duty, and called Tamara at the agency to fill her in.

A few other cars arrived and finally everybody went inside and the thing got under way. This one was mercifully brief. Inside of half an hour the doors opened and the slow exodus began. Troxell was in the forefront, ahead of half a dozen young, beefy guys bearing a simple wooden coffin with brass handles. One of the mourners, a weeping middle-aged woman in black, appeared to be close to collapse. Troxell stood off to one side, watching the pallbearers load the coffin and the weeping woman being helped into the front seat of the hearse. Again, he didn't speak to anyone. A couple of the men gave him curious looks, as if wondering who he was, but no one went near him.

It didn't take long for the cortege to get under way. Eight cars followed the hearse along John Daly Boulevard to the 280 freeway. The first six contained family and friends of the deceased. The seventh was James Troxell, alone in his silver BMW. The eighth and last in line was me, alone in my twenty-year-old Detroit junker.

10

I was there because I was following Troxell. I still had no idea why he was there. Or why he'd attended the two funerals yesterday. All of the decedents seemed to be as much strangers to him as they were to me.

The procession continued down 280 toward Colma, the unincorporated area that abuts South San Francisco, where many of the West Bay's dead wind up in their little permanent pieces of California real estate. Halfway there, my cell phone buzzed. Another thing I dislike is talking on the phone while I'm driving, but I didn't have much choice in the matter right then. We weren't traveling fast enough — a sedate forty-five in the slow lane — for it to present any kind of highway hazard.

Tamara. "This funeral is for a woman named Helena Barline," she said. "Thirty-three, married, no children, resident of Daly City. Killed two days ago in an accident near Westlake Park."

"What kind of accident?"

"Hit-and-run. Red-light runner. One witness."

"Driver caught or IDed?"

"Not so far."

"Witness able to describe the car?"

"Sport job with racing stripes. He thought the driver was a woman."

"No help there. Was she financially secure?"

"You thinking Troxell was her financial consultant? No way. Family was nineteen K in debt — every credit card maxed out."

"Some kind of personal connection?"

"Doesn't look like it. They didn't move in the same circles."

"What'd you come up with on the two women yesterday?"

"Ellen Carswell, thirty-nine, beaten to death by estranged husband in her North Beach apartment. Antonia Ruiz, fifty-two, widowed, shot during a holdup at a convenience store in South S.F."

"Violent crimes. Three cases, three female victims."

"Right," Tamara said. "But that's it on the similarities. Different ages and ethnic backgrounds, income brackets about the same as Helena Barline."

"And I suppose Troxell had no apparent connection to them, either."

"Not that I could find."

"Well, hell," I said.

"Maybe he just gets off on funerals."

"A closet mourner? Better that than some of the alternatives."

"Like talking to aliens or waving his dick at schoolkids."

"Or worse. That death-by-unnatural-causes angle makes me a little edgy."

"Lot of people fascinated by violence and its effects on other folks."

"To the point of attending unknown victims' funerals?"

"Same principle as hanging around homicide scenes."

"Possible, I suppose."

"Anyhow," she said, "the man has no history of violence or mental illness."

"Encouraging, but not conclusive."

"Might be something else in his background. I'm still digging."

"Make it deep," I said, and we rang off.

The procession was entering Colma now. I sighed.

Cemetery — next stop.

There are a dozen or so boneyards in Colma — ethnic, denominational, nondenominational. All attractively landscaped and well maintained, with restful and respectful atmospheres. But not if you've been down there three times in two days. And not if you find the practice of burying the dead personally distasteful. I like cemeteries even less than I like funerals. Cremation and a re-

13

spectful scattering of the ashes in a quiet place is my choice. Kerry's, too, fortunately.

The day before the destinations had been Hills of Eternity and Holy Cross. Today it was Olivet, and that put me in an even bleaker mood. Olivet Memorial Cemetery was where Eberhardt, my former friend and former partner, was interred — the day of his planting being the last damn time I'd been out to Colma until yesterday. The surroundings brought it all back, not only the burial ceremony but the way he'd died and the painful circumstances that had led to his death.

I stopped behind Troxell's BMW and the other vehicles parked along the edge of the road, got out of the car, and walked around at a distance beyond where the remains of Helena Barline, hit-and-run victim, were being laid down. I thought maybe a little exercise, the cold slap of the early June wind, would help me reinter Eberhardt in his memory grave. Wrong. Now that his bones were out, they kept right on rattling. I continued to pace, watching Troxell and the huddled gathering around the gravesite. The wind made enough noise in the trees so that I couldn't hear any of the minister's words or any of the sounds the weeping woman made. But I could see their faces and the movements of their mouths and that was bad enough.

Troxell hadn't joined the group at the grave. As on the previous two burials he stood off at a distance, stock-still the whole time with his hands deep in his coat pockets, his narrow face void of expression. He didn't know or suspect I was there any more than he had the day before. Eyes only for the casket, the mourners, the ritual lowering. It wasn't until the coffin was snug in its grassy plot that he turned away, and then he looked nowhere except at his BMW.

He stayed put until the mourners began filing back, which gave me plenty of time to take position. I turned on the car radio for noise; it helped keep Eberhardt at bay. When Troxell finally pulled away, I gave him plenty of room. He was easy to follow — a slow, careful driver not given to lane changes or sudden bursts of speed. He even flicked his signal on when he made a turn, an act of courtesy that would've gotten him sneered at on most California freeways these days.

So now what? I thought.

Another damn funeral?

No. Not again today, thank God.

Troxell drove back to Daly City, around Lake Merced, and up onto the Great

Highway. Opposite the Beach Chalet at the northern end of Ocean Beach, he swung across into one of the diagonal parking spaces that faces the sea. I followed suit a short distance away. For a time he sat in the car, doing nothing that I could see; then he got out and walked down onto the beach. Not me, not on a blustery day like this. The wind was strong enough to blow up swirls and funnels of sand, and the waves were high and you could hear the pound of surf even with the windows shut. From inside the car I could see a long ways in both directions. The beach was deserted except for Troxell and one other person, jogging with a dog far up toward Cliff House.

He went down close to the waterline, where the sand was wet and the surf creamed up in long fans, and walked back and forth for close to an hour — a couple of hundred yards in one direction and then a couple of hundred yards back in the other. The wind billowed the tails of his overcoat up around his head, so that from where I was he looked like a giant seabird about to take flight. When he finally decided to quit he stood for another five minutes or so, watching the waves lift and slam down or just staring out to sea — I couldn't tell which.

He must've been half frozen when he

came back up to the parking area. But he didn't get into his BMW to warm up; instead he waited for a traffic break and then crossed the highway and went into the Beach Chalet. Crap. That meant I had to brave the ocean wind after all. For all I knew he was meeting someone over there. Someone alive, for a change.

The Beach Chalet has been a San Francisco landmark of one kind or another since the midtwenties. It started out as a fancy seaside bar and restaurant, made even more elegant during the Depression by a WPA artist who decorated its tiled ground floor with cityscape murals. During and after World War II it had fallen on hard times. The local VFW managed it for a while, using it as their meeting place, and when they bowed out the place deteriorated into a hard-core bikers' hangout, then into an abandoned and vandalized eyesore. In the early nineties the city finally decided it was worth saving; the Parks and Recreation Department gave it a facelift and restored the murals and established a visitors' center in the lobby, and the upstairs was rented to an outfit that opened a new-style bar and restaurant attractive to both locals and tourists. Full circle in three-quarters of a century.

By the time I got upstairs, Troxell was on

17

a stool at the far end of the bar with a drink and a twenty-dollar bill in front of him. Straight bourbon or Scotch, a double, no ice. It was nearly two thirty now, and most of the lunch crowd was gone; only a handful of the window tables were occupied, and Troxell had the bar to himself. He sat bowed forward, with his chin down and his eyes on the whiskey. But he didn't drink any of it, just stared into the glass while the bartender brought him his change and served me an Amstel Light draft. At the end of ten minutes he still hadn't touched the liquor, or moved any part of his head or body more than an inch or two.

The bartender noticed; bartenders notice everything when they're not busy. He tried to catch my eye, but I pretended to be interested in my beer and in the decorations over the back bar. He shrugged and washed beer steins.

Troxell sat there like a piece of sculpture for another couple of minutes. Then, all at once, as if he were coming out of some kind of self-induced trance, his shoulders jerked and his head snapped up. He focused on the glass, picked it up, threw the whiskey down his throat in one convulsive swallow, and climbed off the stool and started past me with his eyes straight front.

The bartender called, "Hey, mister, you forgot your change."

It didn't slow him or turn his head. "Keep it."

"There's seventeen bucks there —"

"Keep it," Troxell said again and kept right on going.

The bartender blinked his surprise. He wasn't the only one.

Three more stops for Troxell.

The first was a video store on Taraval. He was in there for close to twenty minutes, and when he came out he was carrying a plastic sack. Judging from its evident weight and bulges, he'd either bought or rented half a dozen VHS tapes. Rather than put the bag on one of the seats, he locked it in the trunk.

The second stop was a combination liquor store and newsstand a little farther up Taraval. His only purchases there appeared to be an armload of newspapers; these went into the trunk with the videotapes. There must've been at least half a dozen. All from the Bay Area? To hunt for more victims of violent crimes, more funeral announcements?

Stop number three, the longest, was a florist shop on West Portal. He spent nearly thirty minutes inside, and when he came out he was empty-handed. Deliberating over a purchase, I thought; found what he wanted and ordered it. Flowers for another funeral? For all I knew at this point, he'd sent wreaths or bouquets to the services yesterday and today — one more facet of his mourner pattern.

From West Portal he drove straight up into St. Francis Wood. The Wood, on the lower western slope of Mount Davidson, is one of the city's best neighborhoods; large old homes on large lots that you couldn't buy for less than a million each — maybe a million-five in the current overinflated real estate market — and at that price you'd have to settle for one of the less desirable properties. Troxell's house was probably in the two-million-dollar bracket. His annual salary at Hessen & Collier, one of the city's more prominent financial management firms, ran upward of three hundred thousand a year and he'd owned his prime chunk of San Francisco for more than two decades — a Spanish Mission–style place, all stucco and dark wood and terra-cotta tile, shaded by pine and yucca trees, flanked by tall hedges. The Good Life, with all its attendant perks. Unless possibly, for some private reason, you were starting to come apart at the seams.

Another silver BMW was parked in the wide driveway; he slid his in alongside. The twin belonged to his wife, Lynn Scott Troxell. I pulled up across the street and down a ways, just long enough to watch him get out and lock his car and enter the house. He didn't take the videotapes or the newspapers with him.

I wondered if that meant he was going out again tonight. And where he would go if he did. Twice a week was his current average for nocturnal absences from home. And very few funerals are held at night.

I also wondered what my client, or rather the agency's client, once removed, would make of her husband's bizarre behavior of the past two days. One thing for sure: it wasn't going to make Lynn Troxell any happier than if he'd spent them in the company of another woman.

2

The central ingredient in detective work is the same as in just about any other business, large or small: the gathering and processing of information. In the old days, before computers and the Internet, you got your information through legwork and personal interaction with people — paying, asking, manipulating, compromising, and often enough, currying favor. Even nowadays there's still a lot of necessary quid pro quo. Ask a favor of somebody, and sooner or later he's liable to request payback. And when that happens, like it or not, you're obligated to say yes.

So I said yes to Charles Kayabalian, a reputable attorney and collector of Oriental rugs who had over the years provided answers to legal questions and thrown a handful of investigative jobs my way. In all that time he'd only called in one favor. I owed him a lot more than this small number two.

Lynn Scott Troxell was a personal friend

of Kayabalian's. She had been in the same graduating class at UCLA with his daughter, and while at the university she'd married her high school sweetheart. The marriage hadn't worked out, and not long after her divorce, which Kayabalian had handled for her, she'd met and married James Troxell. That was as much background information as Kayabalian had been willing to impart; he wanted her to lay out the rest for me, along with her reasons for wanting to hire a private investigator.

"It's a domestic matter," he said, "and I know you don't care for that kind of work. But it's not your typical domestic case. At least, I don't think it is and neither does Lynn."

I met the woman in Kayabalian's Embarcadero Center offices later that day, with him present mostly in the role of observer. She was in her midthirties, dark-haired, slender, very attractive in a quiet and remote sort of way. The first thing you noticed about her was her hands; they were thin and very long-fingered, the bones and veins prominent, the nails cut short and unpolished, and there was grace and strength in the way she moved them — like the hands of a concert pianist. The second thing you noticed was that there was a sadness in her, deep-rooted and as remote as her beauty; you had to look deep into chocolate-brown eyes to see it. Not a recent sadness, not the result of whatever domestic problems she was having, but one long ingrained — the kind of melancholy you'd find in a supplicant who'd lost faith, say, or an idealist who had been irreparably disillusioned. Something had hurt her once, long ago. Her busted first marriage, possibly. Or maybe the cause was nonspecific; maybe it was just life, the long long chain of experiences and day-to-day living, that had done it to her.

Her first words to me were, "I'm afraid there's something wrong with my husband."

"How do you mean, Mrs. Troxell?"

"That's just it, I don't know exactly. He's not the same man he was a few months ago, even a few weeks ago."

"In what way is he different?"

"Erratic, strange . . . not like Jim at all." The long-fingered hands moved together in her lap, lacing and interlacing. "He's a private person, introspective, but we have always been able to communicate. Now I can't seem to reach him. It's as if he's . . . going away."

"You think he may be planning to leave you?"

"Yes, but not as if he wants to. As if . . . I can't explain it. It's a terrible feeling I have, almost a premonition."

"Can you pinpoint when this change in him began?"

"I first began to notice it, little things, four or five months ago."

"So it wasn't sudden."

"Yes and no. I know that's an ambiguous answer, but . . . The specific behavioral changes were more or less gradual, but I think something happened about two months ago that had a profound effect on him. Emotionally, psychologically. That's when he really began to change."

"Can you connect it with any specific event?"

"No. All I can tell you is that it seems to have had nothing to do with me or our friends or his work. Something outside our . . . his . . . normal sphere."

"These behavioral changes — what are they exactly?"

"Moodiness, hours alone in his den, avoidance of social activities. And recently, one or two evenings a week away from home. He won't say where he goes, just stonewalls the subject. The one time I asked if I could go with him, he said he didn't want company."

"How late does he stay out?"

"Four to five hours, usually. From six thirty or seven on. Once last week, until after two a.m. He . . . well . . ."

She fell silent, her gaze moving against mine. Neither my face nor my eyes showed her anything. One of the many things detective work teaches you is how to maintain a poker face. Besides, I wasn't thinking anything yet. No preconceived notions and no quick judgments — that's something else the business teaches you.

I asked, "What else, Mrs. Troxell?"

"Now he's taking days off work — unexplained absences. One or two days a week."

"The same days?"

"No. There doesn't seem to be any pattern to it."

"You said unexplained absences."

"He won't give me or anyone at Hessen and Collier a reason. He just calls in with some excuse."

"Does he stay home, hole up on those days?"

"No," she said. "He leaves at his usual time every morning, whether he goes to the office or not, and stays out most of the day."

"How did you find out he wasn't going to his office?"

"Mr. Hessen, Martin Hessen, called me last week. He'd spoken to Jim about it, but Jim stonewalled him, too."

"Is he letting his work slide?"

"Not to a crisis point, not yet. But of course Martin and the other partners are concerned."

"Have you spoken to your husband's friends?"

"He only has one close friend, Drew Casement — they've known each other since high school. But he hasn't confided in Drew. Or anyone else that I contacted."

"So you have no idea where he goes, what he does during his day and evening absences?"

"Not a clue. I thought of following him myself, but I wouldn't be any good at that sort of thing. That's why I need your services. I have to find out before . . . I have to find out."

I cleared my throat. "Well, there's the obvious explanation for his actions and the behavioral changes —"

"It isn't another woman," she said flatly.

"I'm sure you don't want to consider the possibility, but —"

"It is not another woman."

"I have to say this. It wouldn't necessarily have to be a woman."

"No." Sharply this time. "Whatever is causing this, it isn't love or sex."

"How can you be so sure?"

"I'd *know* if it was. A woman knows. Besides . . ."

"Yes?"

Her hands moved again, joining, unjoining. "My husband has been very attentive to me recently. You understand? Very passionate."

I didn't say anything.

"I know what you're thinking," she said, "but you're wrong. The passion has nothing to do with guilt or subterfuge or even release of tension. It's more than simple physical desire. It's a deep-seated need . . . in some way I don't understand he needs me more than he ever has. The closeness, the intimacy. As if he's trying desperately to hang on."

"To you emotionally?"

"Just trying to hang on," she said.

Just trying to hang on. Euphemism for a man struggling against a mental breakdown. Based on what Lynn Troxell had told me and the two days' surveillance I'd put in so far, that was the most likely explanation for her husband's abnormal behavior. Stress-related, maybe, with the trigger being some disturbing event or experience; or the gradual degenerative result of a genetic flaw or any number of other possible psychological and/or physical factors. Breakdowns happen all the time to all kinds of people, for all kinds of reasons, and manifested in all kinds of ways. More and more every year, it seems; Tamara and Runyon and I had run up against an extreme case ourselves just last Christmas.

Hell, with all the pressures and insanities in the modern world, it's a wonder a lot more individuals don't slide off the edge — great streams of them like lemmings off a crumbling cliff.

It was after four thirty when I got to the new suite of offices in a venerable three-story building overlooking South Park. Jake Runyon was in, sitting at his desk and studying something on the screen of his laptop. Behind him, the seldom-shut door to Tamara's office was closed.

"Hey, Jake. Tamara leave already?"

"No. In her office."

"Somebody with her?"

"She's on the phone."

"Must be important."

He shrugged and leaned back in his chair. He was a big, tense man who almost never relaxed completely, but he seemed to have found a certain comfort level these past few months. When he'd first applied for the job of field investigator eight months ago, his clothes had hung loosely on his compact frame, his slablike face had had an unhealthy cast, and he'd been so tight wound and hard to read that we almost didn't hire him even though he had the best qualifications. Grieving for his second wife, who had recently died of ovarian cancer; alone in the world except for an estranged gay son who had been taught to hate him by Runyon's bitter, alcoholic first wife. The son, Joshua, was the reason he'd moved to San Francisco from Seattle. He'd made some slight progress in establishing communication with Joshua, if not in mending a rift that might well be irreparable. The passage of time and the job with us had helped restore his equilibrium. He looked healthier, he'd put on weight, he wasn't quite so reticent or closed off. The grief was still a powerful force inside him; you could see it in his eyes. It would always be a part of him, I thought, but it seemed he was learning to live with it. We weren't friends — he hadn't made any friends here, seemed not to want or need any — but we worked well together, and respected each other, and in the process we, too, were making some slight progress in communication.

He said, "What do you think of these?"

I leaned over his shoulder to look at his computer screen. Surveillance photos taken with his digital camera. The suspected insurance fraud case for Southwestern Indemnity. "Is that Nicholson?" I asked.

"Helping his brother-in-law move furniture."

"So much for his spinal injury claim. Southwestern'll be pleased."

"I'll close it up tomorrow, then get on the Fisher skip-trace. Unless you need me for something else."

"As a matter of fact, how'd you like to take over the Troxell surveillance, beginning tonight?"

"Okay with me. Troxell's the financial consultant with the funeral fetish?"

"That's him."

"Tamara was working on his background when I came in."

I gave him a quick rundown of the afternoon's events. "Tuesday evening outings seem to be part of Troxell's pattern. I'd stay on it myself, but frankly two full days of funeral parlors, cemeteries, and solitary beach walks are about as much as I can take."

"Sure, I understand."

The understanding was mutual; I wouldn't have asked him otherwise. It had nothing to do with my being one of his bosses or that I was nearly twenty years his senior. It had everything to do with the fact that I had a family to go home to and he didn't, and he preferred working to sitting around his empty apartment. His job was the only thing that mattered to him now, except for his son — the one and only activity he had left that gave meaning and purpose to his existence. I knew all about that kind of obsessive sublimation. I'd been a workaholic loner myself, for different reasons, for a not insubstantial part of my life.

He was writing down Troxell's address when Tamara's door opened and she came out. She looked like she wanted to bite somebody. Her round face — not so round now that she'd shed twenty pounds — wore a scowl that made it seem two shades darker than usual.

"Oh," she said when she saw me, "you're back."

"Few minutes ago. Something wrong?"

"No. Why?"

"That scowl. I like you better with your mouth turned the other way."

"Yeah, well, no smiley faces today. Like the man says, some days the shit comes down so heavy you feel like wearing a hat."

I glanced at Runyon. He shrugged. "Line

from an old movie," he said. "*Body Heat*, I think."

"Uh-huh." I said to Tamara, "Translation into plain English, please."

"No," she said.

"You don't want to talk about it?"

"That's what no means."

"Problem with one of the cases?"

"No."

"Personal, then?"

"No."

My turn to shrug. You couldn't prod her when she was in this kind of mood. I wondered if it had something to do with her boyfriend, Horace; if that was who she'd been talking to on the phone. He'd moved to Philadelphia just after the first of the year to pursue his career as a symphony cellist, and they hadn't seen each other since. Seven months is a long time apart when you're twenty-five years old, in love, and chock-full of raging hormones.

"So the man take you to another funeral this afternoon?" she asked me.

I told her where Troxell had taken me after Colma. "I can't even begin to imagine where he goes on his nights out. Jake gets the dubious pleasure of finding out. He's taking over the surveillance starting tonight."

"What about the Fisher case?"

"My baby, now. I'll get moving on it in the morning."

"Whatever."

"Anything more on the three deceased women?"

Head shake. "Names don't mean anything to the client, either."

"You talked to Mrs. Troxell? You didn't say anything about the funerals, did you?"

"Do I look like my mama raised a backward child?" she said in a teeth-and-bristles voice. "I didn't talk to the woman, I talked to your lawyer friend. Easier for him to feed her the names without getting her all bent."

"Oh," I said. "Sorry."

"Yeah," she said. Then she said, "Troxell's background."

"What about it?"

"One thing I found out, might be important. Happened when he was a kid. Ten years old."

"In Moraga?" That was the East Bay community where he'd been born and raised.

"Right. His best friend was Clark Simmons, same age, lived a couple of blocks apart. Simmons kid's father was an air traffic controller at the Oakland airport — stressed out, drinking too much, abusing his family when he was wasted. He showed up for work drunk one morning and they fired him. So he went home and started taking it out on his wife. Big screaming fight, he started beating her up, she took a kitchen knife and cut him with it. So he went and got his Army forty-five and blew her away. Blew himself away right afterward."

"Jesus. But what does that have to do with Troxell?"

"He was there when it happened, just walked in with the Simmons kid. He saw the whole thing go down."

3

Tamara

On the way home that night she stopped at a Baskin-Robbins on Geary and bought the biggest damn ice cream cake they had. Gooey fudge, whipped cream, about twenty thousand calories' worth. But when she got to the apartment she couldn't eat it. Two bites at the kitchen table, and her throat closed up and she pushed it away. All the weeks spent living on Slim-Fast to rid herself of twenty pounds of flab so she'd feel good, look good . . . good as she'd ever look . . . she just couldn't do it to herself, start eating her way back into Fat City. Not for *any* reason.

She put the cake away in the freezer, wandered into the bedroom. Still some of Horace's clothes in the closet, stuff he hadn't taken with him to Philadelphia. She yanked every piece off the hangers, threw them into a pile in the corner — all except his brown suede jacket, one of his favorites, overlooked or forgotten when he was packing. She found a pair of shears and cut off both sleeves at the elbow, snip snip, slash slash.

Didn't make her feel any better. If anything, she felt worse.

She threw the mutilated jacket on top of the other stuff and sat down on the bed, then sprawled out on her back. Got up in less than a minute and went into the living room and turned on the TV and then turned it off again and shuffled through her CDs and picked one, nothing classical, especially nothing with cellos or violins, and plugged it in and then sat down on the couch. But she didn't listen to the music. Couldn't even hear it over the loop of Horace replays inside her head.

. . . hardest thing I've ever had to do is make this call . . .

Little quiver in his voice, real emotional.

. . . hate to have to hurt you, I'm so sorry . . .

You're sorry, all right, sorry excuse for a man.

. . . there's somebody else, somebody I've known for a while . . .

Lyrics out of a bad old song.

. . . she's a second violinist with the philharmonic here . . .

Sure, that figures.

. . . her name's Mary, she's from Rochester, New York . . .

Do I give a shit who she is or where she's from?

. . . we're in love, crazy in love . . .

Like you and I never were, right?

. . . didn't want it to happen, neither of us did . . .

More bad lyrics, a whole damn chorus.

. . . as serious as it gets, we're going to be married in the fall . . .

Only wedding gift you'll get from me is a gallon of rat poison.

. . . wish to God it could have turned out differently for you and me . . .

Bullshit.

. . . never stop loving you, Tamara, even if you find that hard to believe now . . .

Hard to believe? Try impossible.

. . . want only the best for you, always . . .

Can't say the same for you. So long, you big lying sweet-mouth son of a bitch, I hope Mary strangles you with one your cello strings someday.

She wished now that she been able to say something like that to him, something hard and wounding — gotten in the last word. Instead, her mind a blank, all she'd done was hang up. End of conversation, end of five-year relationship. End of love. With a click, not a bang, from three thousand miles away.

Not that the Dear Tamara call had come

as any big surprise. No word from him in nearly three weeks, two messages she'd left on his answering machine that he hadn't returned. Oh, yeah, she'd seen it coming even with her eyes wide shut. All those months apart, seven long months of no contact except by phone, too busy in her case, too hooked up with somebody else in his, to follow through on plans to spend a few days together in Philly or here.

Saw it coming, sure. But she didn't expect it to come cold like that, him calling her at the agency instead of at the apartment — it had thrown her off balance. Thought he had more class, more courage, than that. Thought she knew him so well . . . how stupid was that? She didn't know him at all. Consider herself lucky she wasn't the one marrying him after all, Mary from Rochester could have him and good riddance. *Didn't want it to happen, neither of us did.* What a load of crap. Back there screwing the second violinist for God knew how long, months probably, while she sat around pining away for him and being Ms. Faithful, putting her own needs on hold, keeping herself pure at heart for her big lovin' man —

The hell with it.

The hell with him.

Fuck men!

. . . Well, now, there's an idea.

More than seven months since she'd done the nasty New Year's Eve/New Year's Day farewell marathon with Horace. Seven months of denying herself, keeping the faith, living the lie. Well, not anymore. Cruise the clubs tonight, pick up the first good-looking guy who showed an interest in her — black, white, Asian, Martian, didn't make any difference — and go to his place or bring him back here and let him hump her brains out. Why not? Horny, wasn't she? Sauce for the goose, right?

She showered, changed into the sexiest outfit she owned, put on her makeup, brushed her hair and dabbed on a little perfume, and went out to the car. Horace's Toyota. Her Toyota now . . . *Keep it, Tamara, I want you to have it.*

She was two blocks from the apartment before she realized, dammit, dammit, that she was crying.

4

Emily was home alone when I walked into our Diamond Heights condo a little past six. Some kind of godawful teen-shriek music poured out of her room, so I knew even before I went in there that she was by herself; one strict rule in the household is that she wears a headset when Kerry and I are on the premises. She was at her desk, working on her computer — which was also the source of the noise being perpetrated by a young female vocalist and a percussive band — and wiggling around the way kids do in time to the assault on her ears and mine. And to think that when I'd first met her, not so long ago, she'd been such a shy, introspective, quiet little girl.

I had to yell at her twice before she knew I was home. She popped the CD out of her laptop, but even in the sudden quiet I could still hear and feel the afterechoes. If she kept listening to that kind of stuff at such a volume, she'd be wearing a hearing aid before she was fifty.

"It's after six," she said in an amazed voice. "Sorry, Dad. I should've put on my headset, but I was surfing the Net and I guess I lost track of the time."

"How can you concentrate with that racket going on?"

"Racket? That's Shannon Stark's new CD."

"Who?"

"Shannon Stark. She plays Holly Grimes on TV."

"Sure she does."

"All my friends think she's major cool."

"What do you think?"

"Well . . . I like others better."

"So you're not going to start singing the way Holly does?"

"Shannon. No," she said seriously, "I don't think so."

So there was still hope for the kid yet. Emily has a fine, sweet voice and singing is one of her favorite pastimes. The thought of her emulating Shannon Stark or any other noisy teenage idol was not a happy one.

"The CD's not mine anyway," Emily said. "Carla's brother downloaded it off the Internet."

"Isn't that illegal?"

"Well, technically, but everybody does it."

"You'd better be the exception. Where's Kerry?"

"She has to work late tonight."

"First I've heard of it. How late?"

"I don't know. I didn't talk to her."

"She didn't pick you up? How'd you get home from Carla's?"

"Um, by bus."

"Bus? You know we don't like you riding buses alone."

"Carla's mom couldn't take me because she had an appointment, so she called Mom and she said it was okay."

I sorted that out. "Kerry said it was okay for you to take the bus?"

"Yes."

"Well . . . how long have you been home?"

"Since around three thirty. I called Mom's office to tell her I was here, but she was in a meeting. I left a message."

"And she didn't call back?"

"No."

None of this was making me happy. It wasn't like Kerry to okay a solitary bus ride, or not to check up when Emily was home alone. Usually she worried about the kid as much as I did — one of the curses of becoming adoptive parents at our age. But she hadn't been herself recently. Working long hours, but I had the feeling there was something preying on her mind as well. And I was afraid I knew what it was.

Emily had noticed it, too. She said, "Mom's been sort of preoccupied and forgetful lately."

I nodded. And broody and not much interested in making love.

"But she's okay, isn't she?"

"Sure she is. Just working too hard."

Emily shut down her computer, stood up and stretched — and when she did that, turning my way, I found myself staring at her. Really seeing her for the first time since I'd come into the room. You expect your loved ones, other people close to you, to look the way they always do, and you don't always notice changes right away. Even normally observant detectives are guilty of that kind of temporary blindness on occasion.

"You're wearing lipstick," I said.

Sheepish look. "Oh, right, I forgot to take it off."

"And makeup. Is that eye shadow?"

"Shadow, liner, and mascara. And a little rouge to highlight my cheekbones."

"You rode the bus alone like that? My God, Emily, what's the idea?"

"Carla and I thought it'd be cool to do makeovers on each other. You know, just to see how we'd look." She gave me one of her big-dimpled smiles. "I think I look about sixteen, don't you?"

"No."

The smile faded. "You don't think I look older?"

"I think you're too young to wear all that makeup, that's what I think."

"Lots of girls my age wear makeup. More than this."

"You're not lots of girls, you're my little girl."

"I'm not a little girl anymore," she said, and stretched again.

"Eleven's not exactly, uh . . . Christ!"

"Now what's the matter, Dad?"

"That sweater. It's not one of yours."

"No, Carla gave it to me. It's too small for her."

"It's too small for *you*."

"I like tight sweaters. They show off my boobs."

"Emily . . ."

"Well, they do. Carla's jealous. She doesn't have breasts yet, she's flat as a board."

I said, "Uh." Then I said, "We shouldn't be having this discussion. . . ."

"Why not? There's nothing wrong with breasts."

"Of course there's nothing wrong with, uh . . ."

"There're nine-year-olds who have bigger ones than I do," she said. "One girl in my class, Tracy Hammer, wears a B-cup bra already. I'll bet she needs a D-cup by the time she's sixteen. And I'll bet they start to sag by the time she's twenty-one —"

"Okay, that's enough on the subject."

"Dad, it's no big deal, really. All women have breasts."

"You're not a woman yet."

"Yes, I am. Technically."

"What do you mean, technically?"

"I've already had my first period."

". . . You . . . what?"

"Last month. It was kind of exciting."

"Exciting. Yeah."

"Don't be embarrassed, Dad."

"I'm not embarrassed," I lied.

"Well, anyway, Carla hasn't had hers yet and that's another thing she's jealous about —"

"Never mind Carla. Why didn't you . . . uh, say something about it at the time?"

"To you? Well, it's not something you just rush right in and talk to your father about."

"No, I guess not. But you . . . Kerry . . . Mom . . ."

"Oh, sure, we had a long talk. About all the other stuff, too."

"Other stuff?"

"You know, sex."

"... Uh ..."

"Safe sex, oral sex, AIDS, and all that."

"... Uh ..."

"I already knew some of it, but there was a lot I didn't know. Mom's so cool, she's not afraid to talk about *anything*."

"Talk ... yeah. Cool."

Tolerant look, the kind Kerry gives me sometimes. Eleven going on thirty-five. "You don't have to worry. It's not like now that I know, I'm going to run out and get naked with some boy."

Get naked with some boy. Gahh.

"We talked about responsibility, too, and waiting until I'm older and I meet the right person and I'm ready for intimacy. I plan to stay a virgin for a long time."

"Well, I'm glad to hear that —"

"At least until I'm fifteen," she said.

"Fifteen! Emily, for God's sake —"

She laughed. "Just kidding," she said, and came over and put her arms around me and gave me a tight squeeze. "I love you and Mom, I'd never do anything to hurt you or make you ashamed of me. Honest. Don't worry."

Don't worry. What, me? Never, no way.

Emily stepped back and let me have another big-dimpled smile. "I'll go wash my

47

face and then get supper started, okay?"
And out she went, leaving me there feeling
as if I'd just run uphill through a minefield.
Why did she have to be so damn candid and
matter-of-fact about everything? Why did I
have to be so damn fumble-headed when it
came to simple parenting skills?

I looked around her room. Stuffed ani-
mals, music posters, Dr. Seuss books, dolls,
old Disney toys, and other remnants of her
former life in Woodside — still a little girl's
room. But there was no denying she'd been
right: she wasn't a little girl anymore.

Makeup. Tight sweaters. Breasts. Bras.
Periods. Safe sex, oral sex, just plain sex.

And this was only the beginning.

Ten past seven, and we were just about
ready to put food on the table, when Kerry
finally showed up. Except for "Sorry I'm
late, there was a meeting that wouldn't die,"
she didn't have much to say. Emily and I
each got a quick peck on the cheek, nothing
more.

I made it a point to give her close scrutiny
over dinner. Normally she looks fifteen
years younger than she is — almost flawless
skin to go with her dark-auburn hair, few
wrinkles and only a scatter of laugh lines
around her mouth. Now, though . . . show-

ing her age a little, the skin not quite as creamy smooth, purplish shadows under her eyes and faint lines at their corners.

Just working too hard? Or was something else bothering her? Cybil and Russ Dancer and Dancer's goddamn legacy, for instance?

When we were through eating she said she had some work to do and closed herself inside the home office we shared. I watched a movie with Emily, not paying much attention to it, and went to bed around ten and read until my eyes began to bother me. Then I lay there waiting with the light on. It was after eleven before Kerry finally came into the bedroom.

"Oh," she said, "still awake?"

"Waiting for you."

"I'm not in the mood tonight."

"Not for that reason. Talk a little."

"About what?"

"When you're ready for bed."

She stayed in the bathroom longer than usual. When she came out she was wearing her nonsexy pajamas, in case I harbored ideas in spite of my denial. She had a smile for me, but it didn't have much candlepower.

"Kerry," I said, "I'm worried about you."

She was plumping up her pillows. The statement made her pause; then she finished with the pillows and got in on her side of the bed and lay back, her eyes on the ceiling. "What do you mean?"

"Just what I said. Something's troubling you."

"Such as what?"

"I don't know, that's why I'm asking."

"You don't want to make any guesses, then."

"Why not just tell me?"

"Good question. Why not?"

I let that pass. "Let's not fence, okay? Is everything all right with you?"

"Why shouldn't everything be all right?"

"You look tired and you haven't been sleeping well. And you've been distracted, moody —"

"You're no barrel of fun, either, when you've been working long hours."

Another pass. "Today, for instance. You didn't let me know you weren't able to pick up Emily. You let her take the bus home by herself, you didn't call to make sure she was okay here alone —"

"Emily's a big girl now. She doesn't need constant monitoring."

"Big girl, right. Pretty, mature for her age. This damn city . . ."

"You worry too much. You're a worry-wart."

"Probably. And you didn't answer my question."

"What question?"

"Come on, don't play dumb."

"Yes, I'm all right," she said, "I'm just on overload. The Hailey account, office politics."

"Nothing else?"

"Isn't that enough?"

"You want to talk about the office stuff?"

"Not really. Not right now. It'll all work out, don't worry."

There was a little silence before I said, "This seems to be my night for being told not to worry."

"Who else told you that?"

"Emily." I gave her a synopsis of our little chat. "Took me by surprise, finding out all that stuff so long after the fact."

"A girl's first period isn't a general topic of discussion."

"I know that —"

"And I didn't give her a sex lecture," Kerry said, "we had a commonsense, mother-daughter talk. Women's issues."

"I understand why you didn't include me. Just as well you didn't. But why not tell me about it afterward?"

"For what reason? It would only have upset you."

"No, it wouldn't have."

"Yes, it would. You're upset now."

"I'm not upset. I'm just saying —"

"Have it your way."

"I'm just saying that I think I have a right to know what's going on with people I care about —"

"Do you tell me everything?"

"What? Of course I do, if it's important."

"Of course you do. If it's important."

"Why do you say it like that?"

"Like what?"

"Implying that I don't."

"What's the matter?" she said. "Guilty conscience?"

Uh-oh, I thought. "Why would I have a guilty conscience?"

"Yes, why would you?"

"I don't."

"All right, then. Can we go to sleep now?"

"Kerry . . ."

She reached up and switched off the lamp and rolled onto her side. In the dark silence she muttered something into her pillow. It sounded like, "Secrets."

"What?"

"Nothing. Go to sleep."

I didn't go to sleep. Neither did she. I lay there in the dark, listening to her thrash around on her side of the bed. Guilty conscience. Secrets. One big secret, more than half a century old and three thousand miles removed.

New York City at the end of World War II. A group of pulp writers, one of the best of them Kerry's mother, who called themselves the Fictioneers and kept the home fires burning with words and booze and pranks. Russ Dancer, hack writer, alcoholic, lecher, and worse, carrying a huge torch for Cybil. And a drunken party to celebrate D-day. One night out of thousands of nights, the wrong set of circumstances — a secret shame buried for fifty-plus years that should have stayed buried and died with the two people who had lived it. Except that Dancer hadn't let it die with him, when he'd finally given up the ghost three months ago. So bitter and corrupt at the end of his life that he'd found it necessary to spew his own brand of venom from the grave.

Kerry must suspect what was behind Dancer's legacy to Cybil, or at least that there was something her mother was withholding from her and that I'd found out about and was also withholding. A small relief, but odd that she hadn't come right out and asked me about it; she'd never been one to avoid an issue, particularly one as large as this one. Sooner or later, she would ask me.

And then what was I going to do? Her mother might be able to flat-out lie to her, but I couldn't. I couldn't tell her the truth, either; I'd given Cybil my solemn promise, and I still agreed with her that Kerry was better off not knowing.

Rock and a hard place, for all three of us.

Damn Dancer's miserable soul.

5

Jake Runyon

He'd been in place, parked in the shadow of a eucalpytus just down the block from the Troxell home, for twenty-five minutes when the subject appeared in the driveway. Right on schedule; the Ford's dashboard clock and Runyon's Timex both read 6:45. He felt a faint stirring, a kind of awakening. When he wasn't working, just waiting, he had the ability to shut himself down — no wasted motion, no intrusive thoughts. Like a machine on idle, waiting to be put to its purpose. He'd learned that little trick during the long months of Colleen's illness, the only way he'd been able to get through the bitter hopelessness of her deathwatch. And he'd continued doing it since, spending a substantial part of his off-time in that twilight mode. It helped keep him sane and allowed him to function; it made his empty life more tolerable.

He watched Troxell walk around to the driver's side of one of the silver BMWs parked over there. Easy man to spot, even from a distance and even without the agency file photo his wife had supplied: tall, lean, long-jawed, wavy black hair streaked with gray at the temples. Still wearing a business suit and tie. He had one of those erect, pulled-back postures, eyes fixed straight ahead, stride long and stiff, completely focused. Not so much different, outwardly, than Runyon himself.

The BMW turned east out of the driveway. Runyon gave him most of a block before U-turning and establishing pursuit. Almost immediately he began to feel energized. On the move like this, with a set purpose, always had that effect on him. Even when he wasn't working, in the evenings and on weekends, he spent much of his time wrapped inside this steel and glass cocoon, taking long drives out of the city, familiarizing himself with each of the cities and towns and unincorporated areas within a hundred-mile radius that constituted his new base of operations. Now that Colleen was gone, and Joshua remained a lost cause, he had no pleasures and only minor interests; work was his single motivation, and a source of almost fierce pride. He was good at it, he craved it; if he could have found a way to exist without sleep, he'd stay on the job 24/7.

Troxell led him straight out Monterey Boulevard to Highway 280 east. Cautious driver during the day, Bill had said; same held true tonight. He didn't exceed the speed limit, observed all the traffic laws. In no hurry, wherever he was going. At the junction with the 101 freeway, he took the exit that led him onto 101 north — heading toward the downtown exits and the Bay Bridge approach. But he wasn't traveling that far. He quit the freeway at the Vermont Street exit.

Potrero Hill? That was it. He took Twentieth Street to Wisconsin, turned there, and climbed the steep incline. Older homes lined it, clinging close together on the hillsides, everything from Stick Victorians to brown-shingled cottages. Prime real estate for the most part, with views of the southeastern rim of the bay. Runyon hung farther back, because there wasn't much traffic and it was still daylight, but the precaution was unnecessary. The BMW's speed didn't vary and it made safe stops at each of the posted intersections.

Halfway up the hill, an even steeper cross street, Madera, dropped away to the left. Troxell swung over that way, U-turned at the intersection rather than entering the street itself. Runyon rolled on past, slowly.

In his rearview mirror he saw the BMW slide in to the curb a short ways down. By the time he found a space on the opposite side of the street, uphill of Madera, the BMW's trunk lid was open, and the subject was out and moving around back there. He adjusted his side-view mirror so that he had a clear view as Troxell withdrew a stack of newspapers and a lumpy plastic sack from the trunk. His afternoon purchases, evidently.

The house one removed from where he'd parked was one of the Stick Victorians, painted in shades of blue, built close to the sidewalk on a lot wide enough to accommodate an adjoining one-car garage. That was Troxell's destination. But he didn't climb the steps to its front door; instead he vanished onto a narrow path that ran in between the house and the garage.

Runyon shut off the Ford's engine, sat waiting and watching. Five minutes, ten; Troxell didn't reappear. He let a little more time pass. Daylight began to bleed out of the sky and the wind, strong up here, grew even sharper; the trees in the area bent and shook in darkening silhouette. Lights were on in most of the homes, but not in the blue Victorian. It remained dark, its lines obscuring as the dusk deepened toward night.

When the last of the daylight was gone, Runyon left the car and crossed the street to the Victorian. There was enough space between it and its near-side neighbor for him to see that the property ran steeply downhill, and that the rear windows were as dark as the ones in front. But there was light somewhere behind and below, a pale glow that spread out from an invisible source. Night-light? Separate building?

He walked past the house, taking his time. Three pot-metal numbers were arranged vertically on one of the rounded porch pillars, just readable in the darkness; he made a mental note of them. The path Troxell had taken was like a short, hollow tube that ended in a wood-and-wire gate set into an eight-foot-high frame joined to house and garage. Nothing was visible beyond it except shadow shapes given faint definition by the diffused light glow. All the windows on that side of the house were dark as well.

No cars on the street at the moment, no one on the sidewalks. Runyon stepped quickly into the tube. The wind made sounds in the night; there were other sounds, too, but they were all muted city noises, none close by.

It wasn't until he reached the gate that he could see what lay behind and below. There was more room back there than he'd expected; an overgrown boundary fence was visible two-thirds of the way down the incline, so that most of the available yard space belonged to the Victorian's owners. Between the house and the fence was a shelf, natural or man-made, and another building squatted there — a low, blocky structure maybe forty feet square, with a door and window on the near side. A set of wooden steps angled down to it from the gate. Granny unit, probably, either built to conform to city codes or put up without permits. One large room or two small ones, plus bath. Nice and private. The light came through the single window, filtered by closed blinds. No way to tell from here if Troxell was alone inside or not.

Runyon tested the gate latch. Locked, of course. You could climb over the frame, but you couldn't do it without making some noise. He was trespassing as it was; no point in compounding the offense. He retraced his steps to the sidewalk, made sure he was unobserved as he came out, and climbed back up to the Ford.

Long wait this time. After a few minutes, he cranked his mind down to basic awareness and just sat there, low on the seat, not moving until leg and shoulder and back muscles protested and then just enough to ease the cramping.

At 10:24 by the dashboard clock Troxell reappeared and walked in deliberate strides to his wheels. Nothing in his hands now; they swung open at his sides. Runyon moved as quickly and easily as if he'd been sitting still for two and a half minutes instead of two and a half hours. He started the engine, waited until the BMW was away from the curb and heading downhill before he made a dark U-turn, then put on his lights and followed.

Subject went home, straight home, following the identical route he'd taken to Wisconsin Street. Runyon parked in the same place he'd waited earlier. It was only after the last of the house lights went off upstairs, half an hour later, that he was satisfied Troxell was in for the night.

Home himself then, a short drive up Nineteenth Avenue to his apartment on Ortega — four nondescript furnished rooms on the third floor of an equally nondescript stucco building. He hadn't eaten since a late lunch, hadn't been hungry enough to bother before tonight's surveillance. He made himself a cup of tea, found half a container of Chinese takeout in the refrigerator. Colleen's drink, Colleen's favorite food. His, too, now. In some way he didn't quite understand he needed to maintain the patterns the two of them had followed when she was alive. Continuity, maybe. Or a way to hang on to the hope that she *was* still alive, somewhere, on some other plane of existence, even though he wasn't religious and did not really believe in either an afterlife or immortality.

He ate at the dinette table in the kitchen, then added hot water to his teacup and took it into the front room. At the secretary desk in there was a copy of the reverse city directory; the agency had a copy, but he liked having his own for situations like the one tonight. The occupants of the blue Stick Victorian had a listed phone number and the reverse directory identified them as Ralph and Justine Linden. He booted up his laptop, wrote out a detailed eight-paragraph report on the evening's surveillance that included the property owners' names, and e-mailed it to Tamara.

6

Jake Runyon

Olivet Cemetery, Colma.

Troxell's second stop on Thursday morning. His first had been the florist shop on West Portal that Bill had followed him to the day before, where he'd picked up a large, white-flowered wreath. He must have been a good customer; there'd been a CLOSED sign on the shop's front door and he'd had to knock to gain admittance. Then he'd driven straight out Nineteenth Avenue to the 280 Freeway and on down to Colma.

Overcast morning, cold, damp from thin streamers of blowing fog. The weather and the early hour combined to keep the mazelike grounds mostly deserted. Only one other car was parked in the section Troxell went to, two-thirds of the way in — a maroon Datsun, no sign of its occupant. Subject parked his BMW a short distance behind the Datsun; Runyon pulled up fifty yards away. He watched Troxell take the wreath from the trunk and carry it in among the graves, moving as if he were passing through a narrow tunnel, eyes front all the way; he seemed to have no interest or awareness in what lay behind or to either side of him. Man with a single-minded purpose — to reach the end of the tunnel and whatever waited there.

For that reason, Runyon followed more closely than he would have otherwise, on a zigzag course among the headstones and obelisks and wooden markers. There were no paths here, all the graves set into barbered lawn shaded by cypress, yew, and palm trees. The grass was slick with dew, and he was careful of his footing. He could feel the cold and damp stiffening his bad leg. Nearly six years since the car accident that had fractured the tibia in three places, forced him to endure two rounds of surgery, and then to take a partial disability retirement from the Seattle PD, and he still had twinges and the slight limp in cold, damp weather. But it wasn't much of a cross compared to what had happened to Ron Cain, behind the wheel when their high-speed fugitive pursuit turned deadly. If he closed his eyes he could still see, as if the image had been burned into his retinas, what was left of his partner lying crushed and bloody inside all that twisted metal.

Troxell had been to this part of the cemetery before, more than once — evident from the fact that he neither slowed his pace nor glanced at any of the markers he passed. He knew which grave he wanted and he went straight to it. Two things set it apart from its neighbors. One was the headstone — larger and taller than most, made of shiny new white marble, with gold lettering and filigree work. Expensive. The other thing was the number of wreaths and bouquets that draped the grave and covered the lower section of the stone. More than half a dozen, all of them of real flowers, not the artificial variety that decorated most of the other burial plots; some fresh, some starting to wilt, one spray of white carnations that had turned brown and brittle.

Troxell transferred the dead carnations to a nearby trash receptacle, then carefully placed the new wreath where the carnations had lain. When he was satisfied, he straightened and stood stiffly, unmoving, his head bowed as if he might be praying. He stayed like that for a long time, the fog wisps swirling around him, as oblivious to the cold as he was to his surroundings.

Runyon was so intent on Troxell and the gravesite that he didn't see the woman until she walked into the periphery of his vision.

His first look at her was brief and indefinite; she came at an angle from his right, and she was wearing a bulky coat, a muffler, and a knitted cap that obscured much of her bent head. He paid some heed to her when he realized she was heading in Troxell's direction, enough to tell that she was young, long-legged, red-haired. But she didn't have his full attention until she approached the grave where the subject stood and halted next to him.

Her presence surprised Troxell; she said something that made him jerk, swing half around. Runyon was moving by then, on the same trajectory. The woman spoke again, but there was enough wind sound to block out the words. Subject's head wagged; his reply caused her to reach out and pluck at the sleeve of his coat. He recoiled as if she'd tried to strike him, said something to her in a raised voice. Part of it carried to Runyon, the words "I'm sorry." Then Troxell spun away from her and hurried back toward the road, bypassing Runyon in a blind rush. The woman stayed where she was by the grave, looking after him — her head raised now, the muffler down off her mouth and chin.

Runyon's first clear look at her was a glance that immediately morphed into a rigid stare. Jolting sensation inside him; his chest tightened, his breath came short. Momentary confusion, a feeling of disorientation, ran James Troxell right out of his head.

Colleen.

She looked like Colleen.

From a distance, in the hazy morning light, she might have been Colleen.

He started toward her, a reflex action so abrupt it brought a twist of pain in his bad leg. In that same moment she moved, too, cutting away across the lawn. "Wait!" she called after Troxell. "Wait!" But he neither slowed nor turned his head, just kept fast-walking to where he'd parked his BMW.

Runyon cut ahead to the flower-banked grave, paused there just long enough to read the inscription on the marble headstone.

IN MEMORY OF
ERIN DUMONT
1980–2005
"IN THE MIDST OF LIFE THERE IS DEATH"

The woman seemed to have realized that she was running across gravesites instead of in the grass strips that separated them; he saw her falter, then slow and shift her route sideways. Troxell was already inside the BMW, a hundred yards away. There was enough time for Runyon to get to the Ford and reestablish pursuit, but he didn't do it.

The woman had halted next to a marble bench, and when Troxell pulled away she sank down on it, unmindful of the fact that it was a memorial rather than a public bench and wet with mist besides. She lowered her head into the splayed fingers of one hand.

Runyon approached her slowly. She didn't seem to know he was there, even after he stopped in front of her, until he said, "Excuse me, miss." Then her head snapped up and she blinked at him.

Up close, the resemblance to Colleen wasn't nearly as strong. Younger, no more than thirty. Face longer and thinner. Hairstyle similar, shoulder length, parted in the middle, but the color was several shades lighter than dark burgundy. Eyes blue, not green, faintly slanted, and liquid with an emotion that he recognized as pain. Mouth wider, the upper lip thicker. Still, there was enough similarity, too much similarity. His mouth was dry. He could feel his own hurt like a fresh probe moving through him.

"What is it?" she said. Voice different, too, pitched lower and not as soft as Colleen's. The blue eyes were wary. "Why are you staring at me like that?"

"I'm sorry. You . . . remind me of someone."

She said, "Oh for God's sake," in a tone of weariness mixed with disgust.

"That's not a line and I'm not trying to pick you up. I just want to talk to you."

"About what?"

"The man you spoke to at Erin Dumont's grave."

Abrupt change in her expression; she was on her feet in one quick motion. Almost eagerly she said, "You know who he is?"

"That's one of the questions I was going to ask you."

"Why? *Do* you know him?"

"I know who he is. I followed him here."

"Followed him? I don't . . . my God, are you a policeman?"

"Private investigator." He flipped open the leather case Colleen had given him as a birthday gift, showed her the photostat of his California license. She studied it — memorizing the information, he thought — before she met his gaze again.

"Why are you following that man, Mr. Runyon?"

"I can't tell you that. Confidential."

"But is it because you think . . . somebody thinks . . . he might have something to do with what happened to Erin?"

"No. That's not the reason my agency was hired."

It was not what she wanted to hear. She bit her lower lip, sank down again on the edge of the bench as if she were suddenly tired.

Runyon said, "Do you mind telling me your name?"

Brief hesitation. "Risa Niland."

"Risa?"

"Short for Marisa."

"Erin Dumont was a friend or relative?"

"She was my sister."

"I'm sorry."

"Don't say that. I'm tired of hearing it from strangers who don't really mean it. You didn't know Erin, you don't know what it's like to lose someone close to you in a terrible way."

He was silent.

After a few seconds, she said more softly, "But you *have* lost someone, haven't you? I can see it in your face."

"What happened to your sister, Ms. Niland? Or is it Mrs.?"

"Not anymore."

"How did she die?"

"Somebody killed her. Raped and strangled her."

". . . When?"

"A little over two months ago."

"And the man responsible hasn't been caught or identified?"

"No. There were no witnesses, no physical evidence."

"Where did it happen?"

"In the city, where else?" Bitterly now. "When I first came out here I thought San Francisco was fascinating, beautiful, a magical place. But it's no different than any other big city — just as dirty, just as vicious."

"What part of the city?"

"The neighborhood where we . . . where I live. Outer Sunset, one of the supposedly safe neighborhoods."

"You shared a place with her?"

"An apartment near Golden Gate Park. Erin went jogging every evening between six and seven. Sometimes in the park, sometimes just around the neighborhood. That night she didn't come home. A man walking his dog found her the next morning, in some bushes inside the park."

"Nobody saw anything, heard anything?"

"Or won't admit it if they did. That's another thing I hate about the city — mind your own business, don't get involved. If it weren't for that bastard still being loose, I'd quit my job and move back to Wisconsin. I swear that's what I will do when the police catch him. If they catch him."

"The man I've been following — you ever see him before today?"

"Once. At Erin's funeral service."

"Speak to him then?"

"I tried to. He avoided me that day, too."

"Possible he worked with your sister, had a relationship with her?"

Risa Niland shook her head. "She worked for two women . . . a women's boutique on Union Street. And she never dated older men. She had a steady boyfriend, a guy her own age she was serious about."

"Name?"

"Scott Iams. He's in even worse shape than I am."

Runyon said, "That marble headstone looks expensive. Did you arrange for it?"

"My God, no. My family and I couldn't afford one like that."

"Her boyfriend, then?"

"Scott couldn't afford it, either. And her employers barely cared enough to come to the funeral. I don't know who paid for that stone. I tried to find out, but the cemetery people . . . anonymous order, they told me, paid for in cash."

"What about all the flowers?"

"Same thing. Every week since it happened . . . wreaths, bouquets. I told the police, but they didn't seem to think it was worth investigating. I do. That's why I came here this morning, why I've been coming here every chance I could the past couple of weeks. The man you've been following, he has to be the one."

"He did seem almost afraid of you."

"Yes, he did."

"Did you identify yourself to him?"

"No. I asked who he was, how he knew Erin . . . just blurted it out. Then I asked if he was responsible for the headstone, all the flowers. He shook his head and said 'I'm sorry,' twice, that damn phrase. That's all."

Runyon was silent again.

Risa Niland said, "Why would he act like that, a complete stranger, if he doesn't have something to hide?"

"There could be an innocent reason."

"Such as?"

"One connected to the investigation I'm working on."

"But you won't tell me what it is. Or who he is."

"I can't. It's not clear yet, anyway."

"Confidentiality." The bitterness was back in her voice. "Professional ethics."

"That's right. But I may be able to help you in another way."

"Help me? Oh, I see. Drumming up business. Well, you can forget it. Don't you think we'd have hired a detective by now if we could afford it?"

"You won't need to hire me. My agency already has a client."

Cynically: "Just how far do your ethics extend, Mr. Runyon?"

"I'm not sure I understand the question."

"Don't you? If you expect something from me besides money . . ."

"Let's get one thing straight," he said. "I don't expect anything, I don't want anything from you."

"Then why help me? Why should I trust you?"

"Helping people is part of my job. I'm good at what I do and well paid for it and I can give you a list of references — others who've put their trust in me and the people I work for."

She held eye contact for several seconds, bit her lip again and shifted her gaze. "Look, I guess I'm just not used to kindness from strangers, even at the best of times. . . ."

"I understand."

"Do you really think you can help?"

"At least to the point of finding out if this man had anything to do with your sister's death. If he didn't, and if he did buy the headstone and all the flowers, maybe I can explain the reasons."

"If you'd do that . . . well, I don't know what to say. Except thank you."

He handed her an agency business card, the one with his home and cell phone numbers; watched her study it the way she had his license before she slipped it into her coat pocket. "You can reach me at either of those numbers, day or night," he said. "I'll need a contact number from you in return."

"All right. But I . . . my home phone is unlisted and I don't feel comfortable giving out the number. Or my address."

He didn't tell her how easy it would be for him to get them. "A work or friend's number is fine."

"Where I work, then. It's a private line." She recited the number. Then, after a few seconds, "Aren't you going to write it down?"

"I have a good memory." He repeated the numbers to prove it.

The wind gusted sharply, blew her hair into a reddish halo around her head. The effect brought a quick, stabbing memory of Colleen standing at the rail on one of the island ferries in Puget Sound, her hair flying in that same sort of wind-whipped halo.

"Is that all then?" she said.

"For now."

"Then I'd better go. It's freezing out here and I'm going to be late for work as it is."

"I'll walk with you to your car."

Neither of them said anything until they reached the road. Solemnly she gave him her gloved hand, and when he released it after two beats she said, "I'd like to ask you a question. You don't have to answer it if you don't want to."

"Go ahead."

"Was I right in what I said before? That you've lost someone close to you?"

". . . Yes."

"A relative?"

"My wife. Ten months ago. Cancer."

Her eyes closed, her face registered pain. Symbiotic reaction. The eyelids lifted again, and she held his gaze for a moment before she turned, wordlessly, and walked to the Datsun and shut herself inside.

He sat there for more than five minutes after she was gone, alone in the brightening morning, not moving, not thinking. More shaken by her and the resemblance to Colleen than he would have thought possible. It wasn't until another car passed on the winding road that he came out of it and used his cell phone to call the agency.

7

Runyon's report on James Troxell's most recent activities and ties to the Erin Dumont rape-homicide case set off alarm bells. The timing was one thing: Troxell's strange pattern of conduct had escalated at about the same time as the murder. It could be coincidence, of course. It could also be that the crime had somehow triggered his mourner obsession, dormant or subdued in him since his childhood trauma. The marble headstone and the ongoing supply of flowers fitted that kind of obsession; it was possible he'd supplied the same service to other victims of violent crime, past as well as present.

It was the other, darker possibility that worried me. Suppose the headstone and flowers were a product of guilt, remorse? Suppose he was the man who had raped and strangled Erin Dumont?

You looked at Troxell's upbringing, the shape of his adult life, and on the surface he seemed an unlikely candidate for that kind of vicious criminal act. Successful financial consultant, home in St. Francis Wood, beautiful wife — good old-fashioned American success story. No history of trouble of any kind, none of the warning flags of aberrent behavior. Normal adult male. Except that "normal" is essentially a meaningless term; any psychologist will tell you that. The human animal is far too complex for any such simplistic categorizing. And Troxell had been witness to a bloody murder-suicide at a highly impressionable age. That kind of shock can create a psychic breeding ground for demons and monsters.

The thing I couldn't quite fit into the man's apparent psychosis, benign or malignant, was the Potrero Hill angle. He might've gone to the Wisconsin Street address to visit somebody who lived there; a girlfriend, despite all the disclaimers. Only he'd done nothing the past three days to even hint that he was anything but a faithful husband. Male friend or business associate, a shut-in he bought newspapers and rented videos for?

But suppose he was the one renting the mother-in-law unit. The obvious explanation for a man setting up a private little retreat didn't seem to apply, so why would he want or need a hideaway? He had plenty of privacy at home; he could do all the newspaper reading and video watching he cared to behind the locked door of his den. A place to keep personal belongings he didn't want his wife or anybody else to stumble over? And what about those videos he'd bought or rented? Slasher films, sick depictions of violence against women?

Getting ahead of myself, jumping to conclusions.

I tried to bounce all of this off Tamara, but she wasn't in a mood for brainstorming. Or any kind of conversation that required more than monosyllablic responses or simple declarative sentences. Over the years a parade of different Tamaras had marched through the agency offices, like a multiheaded Hydra. Most of the heads were likable — Warm and Tender Tamara and Bright and Sassy Tamara were the dominant ones — but a few were exasperating. Today Glum Tamara was back after a long absence, along with her twin sister, Self-Pitying Tamara. Quiet, withdrawn; pinched look around her mouth, puffiness under her eyes that testified to a lack of sleep. Carryover from whatever had upset her yesterday, I thought. I still figured it for Horace-related bad news, and I was ready to offer her a shoulder to cry on, a sounding board to vent at, some fatherly advice, or anything else she might need from me. But the overtures would have to come from her. She'd tell me about it when she was ready and not before. Until then the best way to deal with her — as with Kerry or any woman when she was in a funk — was to do and say nothing to provoke her. Lessons I'd learned the slow, hard way.

I would have to report to Lynn Troxell pretty soon, but not until I was armed with a few more facts to either support or banish suppositions. I asked Tamara to pull up what she could find on the Internet on the Erin Dumont rape-homicide. It didn't take long. One inside-page *Chronicle* news story the morning after the body was discovered, one brief follow-up article, the inevitable angry op-ed piece on the prevalence of sexual predators in modern society, and then silence. Life goes on and so does death, public outcries fall on deaf ears, and after their fifteen minutes of infamy the victims are quickly forgotten.

Erin Dumont had been twenty-five when she was assaulted, manually strangled, and her battered body left in a screen of shrubbery five hundred yards inside the park entrance at Thirtieth Avenue and Fulton. Employed at a Union Street boutique called FashionSense. Born in Green Bay, Wisconsin, moved to San Francisco five years ago — as her sister had told Runyon. Marisa Niland and Erin's boyfriend, Scott Iams, were mentioned briefly.

Longshot that there was any connection between Troxell and either the sister or boyfriend, but worth at least a cursory look. I asked Tamara if she'd run checks on them yet. She muttered something.

"Sorry, I didn't catch that."

"Routine crap," she said, scowling.

"What you found out?"

"What I get stuck with doing half the time around here."

Self-pitying Tamara, rearing her ugly head. Judiciously I said, "Big part of the game, kiddo. Not just for you, for all of us. You know that."

"Yeah, well."

"Risa Niland? Scott Iams?"

She'd run the checks, all right. In one of her moods or not, she was always efficient. Risa Niland was twenty-nine, worked at a place called Get Fit, a health club on outer Geary not far from the apartment she'd shared with her sister on Twenty-Ninth and Anza. Divorced from one Jerry Niland, a Marina district CPA, a year and a half ago. No police record of any kind. No apparent connection to Troxell, personally or professionally. Iams was twenty-six, lived in the Inner Sunset, and was employed by a catering company on Union Street. Single. Likewise no police record except for a couple of speeding tickets, the last one three years ago. No apparent connection to Troxell, personally or professionally.

I said, "Okay. Next question. What did you get on the owners of the Wisconsin Street property?"

"More routine crap. Ralph Linden: forty-six, works for a Japanese company in the East Bay, Yumitashi International. Justine Linden: forty-five, commercial artist."

"How long have they owned it?"

"Sixteen years. Granny unit's illegal — no record of an outbuilding on the original deed, no record of a building permit or application for one since."

"Some leverage in that, if we need it. Anything unusual in their backgrounds?"

"No. Two more of your average San Francisco white folks."

All I said to that was, "Leverage in that, too. People with clean records want them to stay that way."

"You gonna talk to them?"

"Let Jake follow up. I've got some other things to do. See what I can get out of SFPD on the Dumont case, for starters."

There'd been a time when I had several contacts on the San Francisco cops — friends from the days when I'd been one myself, a couple of guys I played poker with now and then, a couple of others whose paths I'd crossed in a friendly way. Time and a series of high-profile screwups, scandals, and shakeups had dwindled their number, and changed the shape and policies of the department. Ed Branislaus had quit the force and gone into private security work in Arizona. Harry Craddock had been promoted and transferred to the Ingleside District Station. Lieutenant Jack Logan, the man I'd known the longest and was closest to, was in line for an administrative position and would probably retire if he didn't get it; either way it went, he was no longer as inclined to do favors for friends and/or to bend departmental rules.

Logan was in and he took my call readily enough, but he was a little on the curt side. We barely got through the how-are-yous before he asked, "So what can I do for you?"

"Some information, if you can manage it."

"Well, I don't know, buddy. You know how things are these days."

"I figured it couldn't hurt to ask."

"Important?"

"Too early to tell. Small chance it could be, though."

"New or cold case?"

"Couple of months old."

"Still open, then?"

"As far as I know."

"Too damn many that are. Which one is this?"

"Rape homicide in Golden Gate Park, end of March. Woman named Erin Dumont."

"Oh, yeah, I remember it. What's your interest?"

"We've picked up a connection to a case we're working. Pretty tenuous right now, no direct link to the homicide itself. But I could use some more information."

"Give it to us right away if the link develops?"

"You know I will, Jack."

"All right. No promises, but I'll see what I can do. Let me have your e-mail and fax addresses."

I recited the fax number and Tamara's e-mail. "Thanks, Jack."

"Don't thank me yet. If you don't hear from me by this afternoon, you won't have anything to thank me for."

One more call, this one to Charles Kayabalian. He was in and he came on the line immediately. "I was just about to call you," he said. "It's been three days."

"Two and a half. This kind of investigation takes time, Charles, you know that."

"Yes, but Lynn . . . well, you saw how worried she is. She called me a little while ago. I told her you'd be in touch when you have something to report. Soon, I hope?"

"Soon enough. Maybe tonight. We're still gathering information."

"That doesn't sound good. Jim *isn't* seeing another woman, is he?"

"Doesn't look like it."

"Don't tell me it's something worse?"

"I don't know what it is yet," I said. "As soon as I have a clear idea, I won't keep it to myself."

"Why the call then?"

"Gathering information, as I said. Specifically, Drew Casement. Mrs. Troxell said he was a close friend of her husband's."

"Of both of them, yes."

"Does he know she's hired a detective?"

"Yes," Kayabalian said. "She confided in him before she came to me. As a matter of fact, he's the one who suggested it."

"Where can I reach him?"

"He owns a sporting goods store in Stonestown. Westside Pro Sports. But I've spoken to him and I doubt he'll be able to tell you much that Lynn and I haven't already confided."

"Worth a shot anyway."

"I don't want to be pushy, but . . . don't keep Lynn waiting too long. She's in a pretty fragile state."

Chances were that state wouldn't improve when I did talk to her again. But all I said to Kayabalian was, "I won't. ASAP."

The connecting door between Tamara's office and mine was open, and when she heard me ring off this time she came over into the doorway. She was still wearing the scowl. "Clark Simmons," she said

"Who? Oh, right, the double homicide when Troxell was a kid."

"Simmons was the other witness. His parents."

"Locate him?"

"For all the good it'll do. He's dead. Twelve years."

"He died young. How?"

"Heroin overdose in Phoenix," Tamara said. "Sent to live with an uncle down there, in and out of trouble with the law from the time he was thirteen. Drugs, vandalism, breaking and entering, car theft."

"Sounds like it might be the result of psychological damage."

"Yeah."

"Ten years old, you see a thing like that happen to your parents . . ."

"Or your friend's parents, same thing."

"Maybe. Hell, probably. There has to have been some damaging effect on Troxell, too. But what kind, exactly? Simple mourner syndrome, or does it go deeper than that?"

"Don't ask me. I'm just a glorified secretary around here."

Another one to let slide by. I pushed my chair back. "Time for me to get a move on."

"Where you off to?"

"To have a talk with Troxell's friend, Drew Casement. Maybe he can give me some insight into what's going on inside the man's head."

8

Jake Runyon

He couldn't get Risa Niland out of his mind.

She rode with him all the way back to the city, a presence that kept interfering with his thoughts and memories of Colleen. The resemblance, the initial shock . . . yes, sure. He understood that. What he didn't understand was the way he'd reacted afterward, was still reacting. Abandoning a surveillance, talking to the woman as he had, the impulsive offer of help, this fixation — none of that was like him at all. Unprofessional, out of character. Disturbing, because he sensed that it wasn't just a momentary aberration he could shake off and forget about. He'd spent months after Colleen's death coming to terms with the rest of his life; established a mind-set and a course of action, his narrow, empty little world arranged and compartmentalized and clearly defined. And now this. All of a sudden, in a few short minutes, something had happened to throw it all off kilter again and he didn't even know what it was.

He forced himself to focus on James

Troxell. Three places he knew of where the man might have gone; his home in St. Francis Wood was the least likely, check the other two first. Potrero Hill was the closest. He swung over to 101, followed the same route to Wisconsin Street the subject had taken last night. No sign of the silver BMW anywhere in the vicinity of the Linden property. He made a quick check of the neighborhood, just in case, and then drove downtown to the financial district.

Troxell had a monthly space lease in a parking garage on New Montgomery, a couple of blocks from where Hessen & Collier had their offices. The location of the space was in the case file: second floor, number 229. And that was where he found the BMW, nose in tight against a concrete pillar. All right. Evidently this was one of Troxell's days to attend to his profession.

He reported this to Tamara. Did she want him to hang around in case Troxell decided to go out again? The answer he wanted to hear was no, and that was the answer he got. She had another job for him, the kind he preferred, the kind that would keep him moving and his mind occupied.

Most Bay Area commuters worked in San Francisco and lived in one of the neighboring communities. Ralph Linden was one of the smaller percentage whose lives were structured the other way around, city dwellers with jobs outside the city — the fortunate types who had a relatively easy daily commute because they traveled opposite morning and evening rush-hour traffic.

The company that employed Linden, Yumitashi International, was located in Emeryville — two floors of a high-rise on the inland flank of Highway 80. The glass doors to the reception area bore a circular logo with the initials YI intertwined in the center; another, much larger logo, this one sculpted of bronze, covered part of one wall inside. There were no other adornments except for a couple of modernistic paintings that looked like original art and several pieces of modernistic furniture. Runyon saw nothing anywhere to indicate the nature of Yumitashi International's business enterprise.

He told the woman on the reception desk that he was there to see Ralph Linden. She sent him down to the lower floor, where he repeated his request to another receptionist there. No, he didn't have an appointment; it was a personal matter. One of his business cards persuaded her to call into the inner sanctum. Before long a fresh-faced young

Japanese woman appeared through a door-way, smiled at him in exactly the same bright impersonal way as the two reception-ists, asked him to wait please, and went back inside with his card. Short wait. She returned in less than five minutes, and this time it was him she took inside.

Two other employees, one Japanese male and one Caucasian female, offered bright impersonal smiles in the hallway; another Japanese male did the same from inside one of the offices. One big happy family at Yumitashi International. Or the smiles were company policy designed to convey that impression. Either way, the effect on Runyon wasn't the one they intended. All the smiley faces gave him an off-center feeling, as if he'd stumbled into a training center for pod people.

Ralph Linden wasn't one of the clones. He was on his feet behind his desk, mouth turned down instead of up, muddy brown eyes behind thick-lensed glasses betraying a nervous bewilderment, when the smiling woman bowed Runyon into his small office. The business card was between the thumb and forefinger of his left hand, the way you'd hold something that might explode. He looked at it again as the woman retreated. When the door closed softly behind her, he said, "I don't know you, Mr. Runyon, I don't understand why you're here. What would a private investigator want with me?"

"Information."

"What sort of information? You mean about me?"

"Not directly."

"My wife? Someone in my family?"

"No."

That seemed to make Linden even twitchier. He was a bulky man pushing fifty, immaculately dressed in a three-piece gray suit, white shirt with gold cuff links, conservative tie. But he didn't wear the clothes well; he wouldn't wear any clothes well. There was a rumpled, ungainly look about him, as if he'd been fitted together out of mismatched spare parts. Wrinkly bald head, long jaw, heavy beard shadow, large ears, thin neck, long arms, big hands with knobby wrists, narrow upper body, broad hips. Uneasy on his feet, too, unlike a lot of big men. Even standing still he conveyed the impression of being loose-jointed, awkward. He would shamble when he walked, and prefer sitting down in any kind of interview or social situation, preferably with something like his gray-metal desk like a barricade between himself and anybody else. He'd relax a little then, be easier to talk to.

Runyon said, "All right if I have a seat?"

"This won't take long, will it? I'm very busy, and the company discourages personal —" A thought seemed to strike him. "This doesn't have anything to do with Yumitashi International, does it? If it does —"

"It doesn't. I just have a few questions."

"Well," Linden said again, and immediately lowered himself into his chair.

Runyon wedged his body into a molded plastic chair that was more comfortable than it looked. The office was a fifteen-foot-square box, neatly kept, the walls painted an antiseptic white, with one small window that faced west and provided an oblique view of one of the other high-rises on the bayshore side of the freeway and a small piece of the Bay Bridge approach. The desk, the two chairs, a computer workstation, and the two of them filled it and made it seem even smaller. Some sort of graph or chart was displayed on a side wall, headed with the words EXPANDING HORIZONS — ironic in this tight, cramped space. He wondered how anybody could stand to spend eight or more hours a day, five days a week, cooped up in here. He'd been in the office two minutes and already he felt claustrophobic.

He waited until Linden was settled. Right — the man was more at ease sitting down. Then he said, "I'm here about your rental unit, Mr. Linden."

"My . . . what?"

"Rental unit."

"You must be mistaken. I don't own any rental property . . ."

"Granny unit on your property in the city."

"Oh, Christ." The words seemed to pop out of him. And he was nervous again, wearing a pained, mournful look in place of his frown. "I knew it. I *knew* this would happen someday. . . . How did you find out?"

"Does it matter?"

"Did somebody report it? Is that how?"

Runyon said nothing.

Linden lifted his hands, held them palm up and stared into them as if he were trying to read something in their crosshatching lines. "It wasn't my idea," he said, "I want you to know that."

"No?"

"My wife, Justine, it was her idea. Her mother didn't even want to move out here, for God's sake. She was perfectly happy in Toledo."

Again Runyon was silent.

"But she had to have her way," Linden said. "Her brother's the one who built the unit, not me."

"Is that right?"

"Ted Mason. He's a contractor, one of those gypsy contractors. He built it himself on weekends and holidays. Oh, sure, I helped him, but what choice did I have? It was the only way I could keep peace in the family."

"Uh-huh."

"I wanted to apply for a permit, but he said we didn't need one. He said there were ways around it as long as none of the neighbors complained. He was right, damn him, but I've never felt comfortable about it. I knew we'd get caught someday." Linden shook his head. "All that money, and she only lived there two years. My mother-in-law. Two years, and Justine found her dead in bed one morning and then what we were going to do? The building was just sitting there, empty."

Rambling a little now in his eagerness to defend himself, shift the blame, self-justify.

"It was Justine's idea to rent it," he said. "I didn't want to go that route, it left us wide open, but we needed the extra money back then. The job I had wasn't nearly as good as this one, and she — Oh, good Christ!

There's not going to be any publicity on this, is there?" He lowered his voice. "Yumitashi is a very conservative company, *very* conservative. You understand?"

"I understand. You don't have to worry about publicity."

"Well, that's good, that's a relief. I can't afford to lose my job, especially in this economy. And I suppose there'll be penalties — fines, back taxes. How much are we going to have to pay?"

"Not a cent, as far as I'm concerned."

"Nothing? But . . ."

"I don't work for the Housing Authority," Runyon said. "Or any other city agency. That's not why I'm here."

Linden stared at him. His eyes, magnified behind the lenses of his glasses, seemed to bulge like a frog's. "Why *are* you here then? What do you want? Money not to report us?"

"I told you, the only thing I'm interested in is information."

"What information?"

"About your current tenant."

"Is *that* what this is all about? You're not investigating us?"

"That's right."

"Well, for God's sake." Relief put a slump in his shoulders. He took off the glasses, pinched and rubbed his eyes before he put the glasses back on. His expression had modulated again, this time into one of chagrin and embarrassment. "Why didn't you say so? Why did you let me —" Then, in a small voice, "You scared the devil out of me."

"Let's talk about your tenant," Runyon said.

"What's he done?"

"He hasn't done anything as far as I know."

"Then why are you investigating him?"

"It's nothing for you to be concerned about. And nothing for you to discuss or even mention to him. Forget this conversation after we're finished and I'll forget what you told me about the rental unit."

"Mum's the word," Linden said eagerly. "Yes, of course."

"To start with, what's the renter's name?"

"His name? You don't know his name?"

"Just answer the question."

"James Troxell. He's a financial consultant, respectable, excellent references, the best tenant we've ever had. Some of the others . . . you wouldn't believe . . ."

"How long has he occupied the unit?"

"Since the first of May."

"He give you any idea why he was renting it?"

"No, and we didn't ask. It's none of our business."

"How did he find out it was available?"

"Well, we don't exactly advertise. We have to be careful. . . ."

"How did he find out?"

"An acquaintance of my wife's works for the same firm . . . Hessen and Collier downtown, she's a secretary there. She told him."

"Did he bring anything with him when he moved in?"

"You mean furniture? No, the unit is completely furnished."

"Phone, television, VCR?"

"Except for those," Linden said. "One of our tenants broke my mother-in-law's TV and wanted us to fix it. Can you imagine? Another tenant made all sorts of long-distance calls and we had the devil of a time getting her to pay for them, so we had the extension taken out. If they want a phone, they have to have it installed themselves, pay for it themselves. Mr. Troxell hasn't, as far as I know."

"Luggage, other personal possessions?"

"I don't know. I wasn't home the day he moved in."

"What about visitors? Any that you know about?"

"I haven't seen any. There's a separate entrance, through a locked side gate, and he has a key. Someone could have gone in that way."

"How much time does he spend there?"

"I really couldn't say. He's there on weekends sometimes. I bumped into him last Saturday."

"Have you been inside the unit since he took possession?"

"No, he's never invited us in."

"And you've never taken a quick look around?"

"Of course not." The suggestion seemed to offend Linden. "We don't snoop on our tenants. What sort of people do you think we are?"

"So you don't have any idea what Troxell does when he's there."

"It's none of our business. Besides, he seems to be a very private person."

Runyon nodded and got to his feet.

Linden said, "That's all then? All your questions?"

"Unless there's anything you haven't told me."

"No, no. I've been as cooperative as I can be. Completely candid." Linden gnawed at his thick lower lip, as if he were considering something. He consulted his upturned palms again before he said, "Is it really important to you, why Troxell rented our unit?"

"It could be."

"Is there any chance . . . I mean, it couldn't be anything illegal, could it? Something that might reflect back on my wife and me, get us in trouble?"

"Anything's possible."

"Christ," he said. "Then we all should know about it. *You'd* know if you saw it, wouldn't you? If you had a look inside the unit?"

"I might."

"In that case I don't see why we should respect his privacy. You're investigating him, after all. The man must be up to something."

Runyon waited.

"We have a spare key," Linden said. "We tell the tenants their key is the only one, but we keep a spare just in case. You never know what might happen. A situation like this . . . well, I could open the unit for you, let you inside briefly, when Troxell's not there . . ."

"You could do that," Runyon said. "It's one option."

"One . . . oh, I see. I could make the key available to you and you could have a look inside yourself. Is that what you mean?"

"It's your suggestion, Mr. Linden, not mine."

"Yes. Well . . . would you tell us what you find?"

"If it's something you need to know, yes."

"I suppose it would be all right," Linden said slowly. "I'll have to talk it over with Justine first, but . . . When would you want the key?"

"If it's necessary, I'll let you know and you can tell me then if your offer is still open. What's your home phone number?"

Linden provided it. "I really should get back to work now," he said. "The company . . . personal matters . . . well, you understand."

Runyon was silent.

"I appreciate you keeping this confidential. About the unit, I mean. And I hope I've been helpful, I hope everything works out all right. If there's anything else I can do . . ."

He'd had his fill of the man. He turned for the door.

"Anything at all," Linden said behind him. "I always like to do the right thing."

9
Kerry

Cybil was waiting at the Cafe Athena in downtown Larkspur when Kerry arrived at 12:25. Five minutes early, and Cybil already had a table and a glass of white wine in front of her.

She didn't see Kerry come in; she was looking at one of the Mediterranean murals that decorated the walls, or maybe just staring off into space, her face in three-quarters profile and apparently lost in thought. Kerry took the opportunity to study her. She didn't look well. She'd always been strikingly attractive, had aged slowly and gracefully; until the past three months, people invariably thought she was ten to fifteen years younger than she was. Eighty-three, now, and she was beginning to look it — the lines in her face more pronounced, a dullness in her tawny eyes, a pale gauntness in her cheeks.

Kerry felt pangs of concern. And a fresh surge of hatred for Russ Dancer. And guilt, too, because of what she was about to do.

But she no longer had a choice. Not any more. It had to be done. If only she didn't have to carry it too far, make it twice as hard on both of them . . .

She steeled herself and approached the table. At her greeting, Cybil jerked from her reverie and put on a bright smile. A mother's smile, a cover-up smile. But nervousness showed in the movement of her eyes, her hands on the tablecloth. She suspected that this was not one of their usual lunch dates, that there was a purpose behind it and what that purpose was. Smart woman, Cybil. Except in her youth, when it came to men.

Kerry kissed her cheek. The skin had a dry, papery feel. "Well," she said as she sat down, "how long have you been here?"

"Only a few minutes. I finished my errands early."

"What kind of wine is that?"

"Chardonnay. Dry Creek. I would've ordered a glass for you, but I wasn't sure about the traffic and the parking. . . ."

"Just as well you waited."

Cybil cleared her throat. She was making eye contact, but not without effort. "You look tired, dear."

"So I've been told."

"You work such long hours. Why don't you cut back?"

"I happen to like what I do. You ought to be able to understand that, if anybody does."

"Yes, but if it exhausts you and makes you snappish —"

"I'm not exhausted. I wasn't being snappish."

"Have it your way then."

She found herself looking at Cybil's glass of wine. It was all she could do to keep herself from reaching for it. Where in God's name was the waitress? "Let's not talk about me. How are you?"

"Oh, well, you know . . . getting along."

"How's the new book coming?"

"Slowly. Very slowly. At my age it's difficult to concentrate."

"You've never had trouble concentrating before."

"Yes, well, it was bound to happen sooner or later."

Finally one of the waitresses appeared. She left menus, went away with Kerry's order for a glass of Dry Creek Chardonnay. Cybil opened her menu immediately and gave it her full attention. Kerry didn't touch hers.

I hate this, she thought. God, I hate this!

They sat like strangers for a length of time that seemed to stretch and expand. The restaurant was crowded; dining noises ebbed and flowed around them. She could feel the tension building, a headache beginning to pulse behind her eyes. Get with it, she thought. The longer you wait, the harder it'll be.

Yes, all right, but not until the waitress comes back with the wine.

"I think I'll have the Moroccan salad," Cybil said.

"That sounds good."

"Everything here is good. You haven't even looked at your menu."

"I've been here before, too, remember?"

Cybil sighed and sipped Chardonnay between pursed lips.

The waitress again, and none too soon. Cybil gave her order. Kerry said, "The same," and reached for her glass. She had to resist the impulse to gulp half of the wine, settled for a large sip.

"Good, isn't it?"

"Fine," she said, and all of a sudden her mind seemed to go blank.

All morning she'd been framing and discarding ways to broach the subject to Cybil, eventually decided the direct approach was best. Not blunt, not emotional, just quietly reasonable. She'd worked out a nice little opening speech, silently rehearsed it a number of times — and now she couldn't remember a word of it. She felt her face start to flush. The wine again, a larger swallow, but all that did was increase the heat until she was sure she was a bright moist red.

Cybil was watching her. "Go ahead and say it," she said.

"Say what?"

"What you came to say. The reason for this lunch."

Open door, unlocked by Cybil herself. But all Kerry could think of to say was, "Why do I have to have a reason to take you to lunch?"

"Kerry, I may be old, but I'm in full possession of my faculties. Something is bothering you — I could hear it in your voice when you called with the invitation. Something you feel more comfortable discussing in public. In order, I suppose, to avoid an emotional scene."

"Yes, something's bothering me. And you know what it is."

"Why can't you just let sleeping dogs lie?"

"Because I can't. Not anymore."

"Why not? Why is it so important to you?"

"For God's sake, don't you think I have a right to know?"

"If the circumstances were different, yes."

"That's an evasion," Kerry said. "I won't

be put off this time — I mean it. If I can't get the truth out of Bill, I'm going to get it from you. Right here and now."

"You believe I'd confide in your husband but not you?"

"Well, he knows. He's a good detective, he must have figured it out somehow. And then he confronted you and you told him the whole story. Is that the way it was?"

"Why don't you ask him?"

"I have. He just keeps stonewalling. Did you swear him to secrecy? He'd never break a promise to you."

"I didn't swear him to secrecy."

"All right, then, it was a joint decision. The two of you trying to protect me. Well, it's misguided. I don't need protecting, I need to know the truth. I've had all I can stand of secrets and lies."

Cybil drained her glass before she said, "I've never lied to you, Kerry."

"Not openly, maybe. Lies of omission are still lies."

"Only if they stem from certain knowledge."

"I don't understand that."

"You want to know the truth. But the fact is, I can't tell you because I don't know myself. Not beyond any doubt."

"Another evasion."

"No, it isn't. Kerry . . ."

"You and Russ Dancer, dammit. You had an affair with him, didn't you."

"I did not. You know how I felt about the man."

"Later, yes. Not how you felt about him during the war."

"I tolerated him then. I hated him afterward."

"After D-day."

"After the war ended, yes."

"Ivan was in Washington on D-day. Did you and Dancer celebrate together? Is that when you slept with him?"

"I would never have voluntarily slept with that man."

"You had other affairs. With that pulp editor, Frank Colodny, for one."

Cybil winced. "Mistakes, foolish youthful mistakes. But never with Dancer. Never."

"Then why were you so upset by that envelope he left you when he died? What was in the letter he wrote you, what was in his unpublished manuscript? What's the real significance of D-day?"

"It's not what you think."

"Isn't it? Cybil, I can count to nine — I was born nine months after D-day. Was Ivan really my father? Or was it Russ Dancer?"

Out, now. All the way out into the open

and lying there between them like the scab off an open wound. Cybil squeezed her eyes shut for three or four seconds. An expression of pain mixed with bitterness changed the shape of her face.

"No!" she said in a fierce whisper.

"But he could be, couldn't he? That's what you've been hiding, you and Bill, these past three months."

"Ivan was your father. Ivan."

"You want it to be Ivan, but you're not one hundred percent positive."

"Ivan, Ivan, Ivan!"

"But it *could* have been Dancer. I can see it in your face." She caught Cybil's hand, held it tight in both of hers. "Why won't you admit it? Don't you understand, I have to know! Today, now, right now!"

Her voice sounded strained, desperate, too-loud in her own ears. Cybil's stare was not the only one directed at her; all the eyes made her shrink inside herself, her skin feel loose and prickly.

Cybil's mouth moved; Kerry could barely hear the words. "Why? Why the sudden urgency?"

Lies of omission, secrets — she was as guilty of them as Cybil and Bill. Put an end to hers here and now. She'd known she might have to; it couldn't be concealed much longer anyway. Come clean as she was making Cybil come clean.

"Medical reasons," she said.

"I don't . . . what do you mean?"

"If there's any chance that Dancer was my father, it means my medical history might be different. Different inherited genes, good and bad. I have a doctor's appointment later this afternoon — that's why I have to know now."

". . . Doctor's appointment?"

"With a surgeon. For a biopsy."

"Oh my God!"

10

Stonestown, off Nineteenth Avenue near San Francisco State University and Lake Merced, was the city's first big shopping mall, built in the sixties to serve west side and Daly City residents. In its early years it had been open-air, with shops off a central courtyard and side ells that were like arctic tundras whenever the wind and fog came howling in off the ocean. As a result the flow of shoppers dwindled steadily and a number of businesses closed down. The entire mall probably would have shut down in the late eighties, if it hadn't been for a group of developers who took it over and spent millions renovating and enclosing it. All sorts of new retail blood poured into the new Stonestown Galleria, including department stores and chain stores, and the shoppers came back in droves. It had been a thriving operation ever since, and despite high rents, that meant a long waiting list for available space. However long Drew Casement had been in business there, he must be doing pretty well to keep on meeting his monthly nut.

Westside Pro Sports was a large, deep space along one of the short side ells. In keeping with the time of year, most of the upfront displays were of summer pursuits: baseball equipment, golf paraphernalia. The rest of the store was crowded with fishing and hunting apparatus, half a dozen customers, one twenty-something clerk earnestly trying to sell an item called a subcontinental adventure travel pack to a dubious teenager, and a sun-browned, well-set-up guy in his late thirties marking down prices on a rack of pro football jerseys. I figured the tanned guy for Drew Casement — right age, and a walking advertisement for the healthy sporting life — and that was who he was.

Casement was expecting me; I'd called from the office to make sure he was in before driving out here. He didn't waste any time after I identified myself. Just pumped my hand once, said he was glad to meet me, and led the way into a cluttered private office at the rear.

No wasted time in there, either. He said as soon as he shut the door, "What've you found out about Jim? Is it another woman?"

"That's doubtful," I said.

"Doubtful? Then you're not sure?"

"We're reasonably sure it isn't."

"What's going on then? What's the matter with him?"

"I can't say, Mr. Casement."

"Can't or won't?"

"Both. My reports go directly to my client, no one else."

"Lynn and I don't have any secrets."

"Then you can get the details from her when the time comes."

"You haven't told her anything yet?"

"There's nothing definite to tell at this point. That's why I'm here. Gathering information, trying to piece things together."

He ran a hand over his face. He was clean-shaven, but he had a heavy beard shadow; longish fingernails made a faint rasping noise in the bristles, like the wheeze of an asthmatic. "I'm sorry," he said, "I didn't mean to push myself at you. It's just that I'm worried about Jim. Lynn, too."

"Sure. Understood."

"I'll help in any way I can, but . . ." He made a helpless gesture. "If I knew anything I'd've told Lynn right away. Jim is . . . well, he's shrink-wrapped."

"How's that again?"

"Oh, you know, not a guy who'll open up to anybody about anything, even his wife. She must've told you that. Sometimes you have to work just to get him to talk about sports or the weather."

"You've known him since high school, is that right?"

"Right," Casement said. "Senior year at Lafayette High. His family moved over there from Moraga the summer before. He didn't have any friends, never made friends easy. Funny, in a way, that the two of us ever hooked up."

"How so?"

"I was a jock back then — football, baseball. One of the cool crowd, lots of chicks, always partying. I didn't study much and my grades got so low I came close to being declared academically ineligible partway through football season. Jim . . . well, he was the nerd type. Smart, real smart. His best subjects were my worst: history, math. So I asked him to help me out, and he did."

"Tutored you."

"That's it. Once we got to know each other, spent some time together, we hit it off. The old opposites thing, I guess. He was never easy to talk to, but once you got past his . . . what's the word?"

"Reticence?"

"Yeah, reticence. Once you got past that he still didn't say much, but what he did say made sense. He helped me and I helped him. He'd always been a loner, shy, still a virgin in his senior year." Casement grinned. "I took care of that little problem for him. Got him some dates, got him laid more than once before graduation."

"Did he ever say anything about his childhood?"

"You mean what happened with his friend's parents? No. Never. I asked him about it once, and he just wouldn't deal with it."

"How did you find out?"

"I don't remember exactly," Casement said. "It wasn't a secret or anything and I guess somebody mentioned it — my old man, maybe, he was always going on about violence in our society."

"Do you know if Troxell ever talked to his wife about what happened?"

"If he did, she never mentioned it to me. You think that could have something to do with the way Jim's acting now?"

"It's possible. Do you?"

"Well . . . it happened so long ago, more than twenty-five years."

"Some people never get over that kind of shock."

"Yeah. I can see that."

"A few develop a kind of morbid preoccupation with death," I said.

"Is that right? How so?"

"They think about it constantly. Read and talk about it. Develop obsessive interests in violent crime. Attend funerals, even the funerals of strangers."

"None of that sounds like Jim."

"He never expressed or exhibited any particular interest in violent crime?"

"Not to me. I mean, the subject's come up, sure, how can you avoid it these days? He hates all that crazy shit, same as I do. But he puts the blame on the wrong horse. Only serious argument we ever had was over gun control."

"So you'd say he's strongly anti-violence?"

"Absolutely. Bleeding heart, victims' rights type of guy."

Like me. But all I said was, "Nonviolent himself."

"Oh, sure. Jim wouldn't hurt a fly. At least . . ." Casement paused. "What about the idea of suicide?"

"What about it?"

"That's another sign of preoccupation with death, isn't it?"

"It can be. Why?"

"Well, something Jim said to me when we were having the gun control argument. I just remembered it. I said suppose somebody at-

116

tacked him, could he kill in self-defense. He said, 'No, the only person I could ever kill is myself.' "

"Did you ask him about it?"

"You bet I did. Something like 'Don't tell me you've thought of knocking yourself off.' He said yes, he'd entertained the notion. Those were his exact words, entertained the notion. He meant it, too. He wasn't kidding around."

"Did he elaborate, give you a reason?"

"Uh-uh. I said, man, you've got everything to live for — beautiful wife, money, nice home, great job — why would you ever think about a thing like that? He just shook his head and changed the subject."

"Did it ever come up again?"

"No," Casement said. "Christ, that couldn't be it, could it? What's going on with him now?"

"Let's hope not."

"But if it is, why now all of a sudden?"

"There'd have to be some kind of provocation," I said. "Even people who've thought about suicide over a long period of time don't suddenly decide to do away with themselves."

"You mean something has to push them into it."

"A trigger, yes."

"What would do it?"

"Severe shock, emotional upheaval."

"Something he saw? Like when he was a kid?"

"Why do you say that?"

Casement said, "A few weeks ago, right around the time he started acting weird, I stopped by their house and he was even quieter than usual. I asked him what was wrong. He said, 'I saw something, Drew.' I asked him what'd he seen. He wouldn't say. All he'd say was 'I wish to God I'd gone straight home that night.' "

"Those were his exact words?"

"Near as I can remember."

"He give you any idea which night he meant?"

"No."

"Or where he was or had been that night?"

"Uh-uh. Just closed right up again."

"But you're sure the conversation took place a few weeks ago? Late March, early April?"

"Had to've been right around the first of April."

"Was his wife there at the time?"

"Not in the room with us, no."

"Did you say anything to her about what he'd said?"

"I meant to, but I didn't. Didn't seem all that important, went right out of my mind."

"And he didn't bring it up again?"

"I'd remember if he had."

11

Tamara

Horace called the office again at one thirty.

"Tamara, listen to me, please. I didn't sleep much last night, haven't been able to stop thinking about how we left things yesterday. I can't stand the idea of you hating me, after everything we had together. Can't we —"

That was as far as she let him get before she banged his ear.

She thought about putting the answering machine on in case he called back. Didn't do it. Didn't want to hear his voice again. Damn the man! He'd gone and hooked up with Mary from Rochester, he was through with Tamara from San Francisco and she was through with him, why couldn't he just leave her be so she could get on with her life?

Until his call, some numbness had started to set in. Hadn't been an easy morning with Bill hanging in the office, giving her the kind of looks Pop used to — you couldn't keep anything from that man, not for long. Word! What she needed today wasn't paternal understanding, what she needed was to be left alone. Better after he went on out. Not as much trouble concentrating, able to throw herself deep enough into her work to keep her mind off Horace and the sorry state of her love life. Everything was humming along on the professional side — they'd have to hire another investigator if their caseload got much heavier — and then all of a sudden the personal side turns to shit. And wasn't that always the way with her? Get one part straightened out and running smooth, and bang, something else screws up. Like she was cursed or something. Like somebody somewhere kept making voodoo Tamara dolls and sticking pins in them.

The phone didn't ring again.

Yeah, but Horace wouldn't give up. Fool would call again, here or at the apartment, and keep on trying to punk her. She knew him so well . . . that side of him anyway. Stubborn. Once he got an idea in his head, you couldn't yank it out with a pair of pliers. And the idea now was to get her to say okay, sure, I forgive you, big guy, let's be friends, and then he'd feel better about himself and what he'd done and go on doing the nasty with his Mary from Rochester with a clear conscience. Well, it wasn't gonna happen. No way. She'd keep right on banging his ear until he let her be, no matter how long it took.

Now she was restless. She paced around her office and the anteroom, stared out through the windows at South Park, paced some more. Lord, she wished she'd gone through with her plan last night, made the club scene and picked up some guy and humped the night away. Sexual frustration was part of her problem, no question about that. But she hadn't been able to do it. Got all the way over to the Mission, drove around looking for a parking place, and the next thing she knew she was on her way back home. Hadn't even thought about it, just drove back to the apartment and dragged that ice cream cake out of the freezer and ate half of it in about two minutes flat. And then she'd gone into the bathroom and puked it up like some bulimic teenager.

Too soon after the Dear Tamara call, that was one reason she'd blown off the club crawl. A knee-jerk reaction to sudden trouble wasn't like her; she'd outgrown the impulsive behavior that'd gotten her messed up more than once when she was younger. Another reason was that maybe she'd outgrown casual sex, too. As much as she wanted to get laid, she didn't really want it to be with some stranger who didn't have a clue who she was or care any more about her than she would about him. Being with one man for so long had changed her outlook, turned her into the same sort Bill was and Jake had been when his second wife was alive. Monogamous. Wanting more than just an orgasm out of a sexual relationship — needing closeness and caring and understanding and some mutual respect.

Like she'd had once with Horace.

Like he was having with Mary from Rochester.

Then go find somebody else, girl. Easy as pie, right? Put an ad in the newspaper, sign up with an Internet dating service, join a church group. Mr. Right's out there someplace, just waiting for Ms. Right to come along. Can't take more than a few weeks, a few months, a few years at the outside.

Got a better idea, she thought. Go out tonight after work and buy some new batteries for that vibrator of yours. May not be the perfect solution, but at least Mr. V's an old and caring friend and besides, you won't have to talk to him afterward or look him in the eye when you wake up in the morning.

Behind her, the phone bell went off. Fax line this time; the bell made a different sound. She stayed by the window, watching a group of young kids playing on the swings and slides on the little playground below, until the transmission was finished. Then she went over and gathered up the half-dozen sheets from the tray. SFPD computer printouts on the Erin Dumont rape-murder, no cover note.

She'd just finished going over them at her desk when the phone rang again, main line. Boss man checking in.

"Jack Logan came through," she told him. "Homicide inspectors' reports and coroner's report, both."

"I figured he would. Anything that didn't get into the media?"

"Plenty. Erin Dumont wasn't attacked and killed where her body was found. No forensic evidence at the site or on her clothing. Lacerations and a few fibers on her buttocks and legs consistent with rough upholstery material, like a car seat."

"Forced into a car and driven somewhere else."

"Or got in willingly with a guy she knew. Question is, why didn't he leave the body where he did her? Had to be pretty isolated, wherever that was. Why risk bringing it back and dumping it near where he picked her up?"

"Good point," he said. "If the vicinity of

Thirtieth and Fulton is where he picked her up."

"She went jogging in that area every weeknight, according to her sister — in and out of the park."

"Well, she could've changed her routine for some reason without telling the sister."

"Could have, yeah."

"But you don't think so. What's the rest of it?"

"She was already dead when he raped her," Tamara said.

"Jesus."

"Violent sexual assault, vaginal tearing but almost no blood. Blood on her face, though — busted nose, skin torn by something sharp-edged like a ring. She might've been unconscious when she was strangled."

"Small mercy if she was."

"Finger marks on her throat indicate a man with big hands, strong. Her windpipe was crushed. But she put up a fight first. Marked him. Skin and blood under all the fingernails on her right hand."

"No DNA match yet, obviously."

"No."

"So he's either a first-time offender or a repeater who's never been caught. They find semen or did he use a condom?"

"Semen. But that's not all. Tear tracks on her breasts and belly."

"*Tear* tracks?"

"He put his head down on her and cried afterward. Cried for a long time — large sections of her skin smeared with dried tears."

The line hummed in her ear for a time before Bill said, "Sudden remorse doesn't fit the profile of a violent predator."

"Neither does this: he put her clothes back on before he dumped her."

"All her clothes?"

"Everything, including panties and bra. Dressed her real neat, the report says. Laid her on her back on a grass patch inside those bushes, folded her hands across her chest." Tamara paused to lick moisture over dry lips. Reading and then repeating the words in the reports had built a dry, hot, impotent fury in her. "Sick motherfucker," she said.

"Psychotic. You see that kind of thing in serial profiles."

"Doesn't sound like a serial to me."

"You don't believe she was a random victim?"

"No condom, those tear tracks, putting her clothes back on, taking her back near where she lived, laying her out. Obsessive love-hate shit. Somebody who wanted *her,* nobody else."

"Stalker?"

"Kind she knew about or the kind she didn't."

"SFPD figure it that way?"

"No mention in the reports. Inspectors interviewed her boyfriend, some other friends, neighbors, the people she worked with. If there was anything along the stalker lines, they missed it."

"Or didn't ask the right questions."

"Yeah."

"Well, I don't see Troxell as the perp. No indication he ever knew Erin Dumont, and his wife couldn't help but notice if he'd been marked. But it's possible he's linked in another way."

"What way?"

"Witness," Bill said. "Either to the abduction or to the dumping of the body. His friend Casement told me Troxell saw something that disturbed him pretty badly, and the timing is right. All Troxell would say about it was that he wished to God he'd gone straight home that night."

"If he did see something, why didn't he go to the cops?"

"The usual reason — didn't want to get involved. Maybe he didn't see enough to be sure of what was happening, didn't get a license plate number, couldn't describe the man or the car. Rationalized it that way."

"So he reads about it in the papers next day, feels guilty, and starts sending flowers and pays for Erin Dumont's headstone."

"It could also be the basis for his obsession with victims of violent crimes, funerals, all the rest of it. Makes sense psychologically."

Tamara said, "Suppose he did see something that'd lead the cops to the perp? Suppose he's been keeping it to himself all this time?"

"Everything about him says he's a responsible citizen, but if he is holding back, then he's a lot more damaged than we suspected."

"So what do we do?"

"Just what we've been doing. We can't alert the police without some kind of proof of his involvement. Where's Jake now?"

"On his way back from seeing Ralph Linden."

"And?"

"Troxell's the one renting the granny unit. Jake can get in if we want him to go ahead. Linden offered him a spare key."

"Offered being the operative word?"

"That's what Jake said."

"Does he have the key yet?"

"No. Shouldn't take more than a phone call."

Bill chewed on that for a time before he said, "There may not be anything to find. Then again there may be more in that unit than we're bargaining for. It's a risk either way."

"Only one way to find out. Won't be the first time a law got broke in a good cause." Like last spring, when she'd got herself into the mess in San Leandro and Bill and Jake had had to commit a B & E on the way to helping her out of it. But she didn't say anything about that. Didn't want to think about it. Those twenty-four hours still gave her nightmares.

"Bent, not broke. There's a subtle distinction."

"Uh-huh. Tell him to go ahead?"

"As far as setting it up with Linden for the key. Before we go any further than that, let's see what Troxell does tonight."

"You want Jake to keep up the surveillance?"

"No, I'll take it. That'll leave him free to do the bending if it works out that way. Meanwhile he can follow up on the stalker angle — talk to Erin Dumont's sister, boyfriend, friends, the people she worked with."

Tamara sat quiet for a time before she called Runyon. Her throat felt clogged up, as if she'd swallowed a bone. Images conjured up by the reports moved dark and ugly across the screen of her mind; she'd never laid eyes on Erin Dumont alive or dead, didn't even know what the woman looked like, yet she could almost feel her terror and pain that last night of her life. Always been against the death penalty in principle, but whenever she came up against one of these inhuman scumbags, all her liberal attitudes went slipping and sliding away. This rape-homicide case, even though there was no personal connection, was having the same effect on her as the near-lethal encounters with the lunatic gunman last Christmas, the kid-abductor this past spring. Stalkers, rapists, child molesters, all the sadistic predators who preyed on women — they were the criminals she hated most. Lethal injection wasn't enough for them. Every first-time offender convicted of a violent sexual crime ought to have his genitals whacked off; then there wouldn't be any repeat offenders. If they used their dicks as weapons, they didn't deserve to keep them. Why wasn't that the goddamn law anyway? Because men made the laws. Cruel and unusual punishment, they said, the same self-righteous, pious bastard politicians who wanted to repeal the abortion laws and let women start dying again in agony and shame in back-alley rooms. What the hell was that if not cruel and unusual punishment?

Real easy, she thought bitterly, to understand why some women hated men, all men. Be real easy right now for her to count herself among that sisterhood.

12
Jake Runyon

Scott Iams, Erin Dumont's boyfriend, worked for a catering company on Union Street on the edge of Cow Hollow — one block from the boutique FashionSense, where she'd been employed. Upscale neighborhood, mostly residential, tucked between Pacific Heights and the Marina, so named because city farmers and ranchers had kept dairy and beef cattle there during the Gold Rush years. Choice real estate nowadays, the kind of district where young, unskilled people worked and counted themselves lucky for their above-average salaries, but still couldn't afford to live.

Iams was twenty-four, red-haired, linebacker-sized. He had the kind of face that would normally be good-natured, easygoing, but that was marked now by the filaments of tragedy. His blue eyes were mournful, his manner dull and listless. Runyon's name and ID stirred up a little animation but no surprise; Risa Niland had called him earlier, he said, told him about her meeting with Runyon at the cemetery and his offer of help. He had a break coming and suggested they go for a walk while they talked. "I can't seem to sit still since it happened. Seems like I have to be moving all the time, even in the middle of the night."

Outside, Iams set a fast, long-striding pace that Runyon had to work to match. It was cold and windy here, this close to the bay, and there were twinges again in his bad leg. Exercise was good for the rebuilt bone and muscle; he'd learned to relish the pain, convert it into positive energy.

Iams said, "I don't know what I can tell you, Mr. Runyon. Some nights I'd go jogging with Erin, but that night I had to work late. That night of all nights. Jesus, it makes me half crazy every time I think about what she must've gone through. I loved her, you know? I mean I really loved her."

"How long had you been dating?"

"Six months, about. We met at Perry's, that's a bar up the street. We hit it off right away. I don't believe in love at first sight or anything like that, but this was pretty close. You know?"

"Was she seeing anybody else at the time?"

"Not really. She had a lot of dates, she was so beautiful . . ." His voice caught on the last two words; he shook his head and repeated them, more to himself than to Runyon this time. "So beautiful."

"Any steady boyfriends before you?"

"A couple, sure."

"Relationships end on friendly terms?"

"As far as I know."

"Was there anybody she had problems with?"

"Problems?"

"Men she dated who came on too strong, men she rejected who wouldn't take no for an answer, kept bothering her?"

"Cops asked me that, too."

"And?"

"I don't think so," Iams said.

"But you're not positive?"

"She'd've told me if there was."

"It wouldn't have to have been recently. Before she knew you, at any time."

"No, she'd've told me. We told each other everything about ourselves. That's how serious it was getting between us . . . ah, Jesus. Jesus. Why her? Of all the people in this city, why Erin?"

There was nothing for Runyon to say to that.

Iams said, "I've been thinking the guy must've been a stranger, one of those crazy random things. But I guess he could be somebody she knew. And he wouldn't've had to be hassling her, right?"

"Not necessarily."

There was a little silence before Iams said, "Fatso."

"Who would Fatso be?"

"A guy who was hanging around her for a while. But it couldn't be him."

"Why couldn't it?"

"Well, it was a couple of years ago, before we hooked up. And he didn't hassle her, not the way we've been talking about."

"What did he do?"

"Just kept showing up, following her around like a big fat dog."

"Is that the phrase Erin used, a big fat dog?"

"Yeah. She said he was humongous."

"How big is humongous?"

"Three hundred pounds or more."

"Where was it he kept showing up?" Runyon asked. "In this neighborhood? Where she lived? Someplace she went regularly?"

". . . I don't know. All she said was he was around for a while and then he was gone, like maybe the Animal Control people came and carted him off to the pound. She thought it was funny. She was laughing when she told me about him."

"What was his real name?"

"All she called him was Fatso."

"She know what he did for a living?"

"If she did, she didn't say."

"He followed her around, you said. Literally?"

"I don't think she meant it like that," Iams said. "Just that he kept turning up places she went."

"Did he approach her, strike up a conversation?"

"Hi, how are you, that kind of stuff."

"Ask her to go out with him?"

"Once. She blew him off."

"How did she blow him off?"

"How?"

"Cut him short, let him down easy, laugh at him?"

"She didn't say anything about that. But Erin . . . she wasn't a cruel person. She made jokes about him, sure, but she wouldn't've done it to his face."

"How did he take the rejection?"

"Like it was what he expected. Went off with his tail between his legs, Erin said."

"Did he keep coming around after that?"

"I think maybe once or twice."

"How long altogether?"

"Not very long. Maybe a month."

"Then he just disappeared? No reason or provocation?"

"Nothing she said or did, no. There one day, gone the next."

"Did she see him again after that?"

"No. Erin said they probably put him to sleep at the pound because nobody would want to adopt him, he'd cost too much to feed. She was really pretty funny, all that dog stuff."

"Sure," Runyon said. "Funny."

"He couldn't be the one, could he? I mean, he never really bothered her or anything. And it's been a long time . . ."

"Do you know if Erin told her sister about this man?"

"Well, she probably did. They were close."

"How about girlfriends she might have confided in? Or who might've been with her when Fatso was hanging around?"

"Well . . . she had a lot of friends, and I don't know all of them. Risa could tell you better than I can."

"I'll ask her," Runyon said. "One more thing. Did you tell the homicide inspectors about Fatso?"

"Yeah, I did. But they didn't ask nearly as many questions as you did."

Which meant they didn't see much in it

and wouldn't have spent a lot of time on the lead. Maybe they were right. And maybe they weren't.

The two women who owned FashionSense had nothing to tell him. At first there was a pretense of restrained cooperation, but after a handful of questions it was plain that they resented the intrusion. One of them, Joy Something, a sleek blonde in her early thirties, ended the pretense finally by saying, "Oh, Lord, we don't *know* anything about what happened to Erin, if we did we'd have told the police. We've answered these same questions so many times already. Really, it's becoming tedious."

"Tedious," Runyon said flatly. "A young woman who worked for you was brutally raped and murdered less than two months ago, the man responsible still hasn't been identified, and you find the investigation tedious."

The other woman, dark-haired, Tess Something, said, "For heaven's sake, Joy didn't mean it that way."

"Of course I didn't," Joy Something said. "We're not insensitive people. But you have to understand our position, Mr. . . . . what was your name again?"

"Runyon."

"Mr. Runyon. Policemen and now a private detective trooping in and out, asking questions . . . it isn't good for business. We're just making ends meet as it is, and the landlord is threatening to raise our rent again. . . ."

"Who hired you anyway?" Tess Something asked. "Erin's sister?"

He just looked at her.

"I didn't think she had enough money. And besides, what can you do that the police haven't?"

"We'd help if we could," Joy Something said. "We liked Erin, she was a pleasant girl, a good employee, what happened to her was a terrible thing, but we just don't know anything."

"Nothing at all."

"And we do care, even if you don't think so."

"But you can only grieve for someone so long, especially someone you didn't really know well. Life has to go on. You can't expect us to put ours on hold."

Runyon still didn't trust himself to speak. He put his back to them and walked out, fast, before the anger in him boiled over and he said or did something he would later regret.

Risa Niland said, "Fatso? Yes, I remember Erin mentioning him. But that was two years ago, and she didn't have any trouble with the man."

On the phone her voice sounded lower, with some of the same huskiness as Colleen's. Imagination? He tried not to focus on it as he said, "Are you sure about that?"

"She'd have told me if she had."

"What did she say about him, exactly?"

"Just that he was worshipful, like a big dog. She laughed about it."

"Did she say where and how she'd met him?"

"Let me think. . . . In the park somewhere, the first time. Stow Lake? Yes, Stow Lake. She was there with one of her girlfriends and he came up and spoke to her. I guess it surprised her."

"Why is that?"

"Well, he weighed three hundred pounds."

"You saw him yourself?"

"No, that's what Erin said. I never saw him."

"Did she describe him in any other way?"

". . . Yes. Long hair in a ponytail."

"What color?"

"I don't remember her saying."

"Age?"

"Around her age. Not much older or she wouldn't have found him so amusing. She had a thing about older men hitting on her."

"Anything else you can tell me about him?"

"Apparently he was shy and stumbled over his words. Afraid of rejection, I suppose. He must have had a lot of it in his life. Oh, and she said he looked silly in his uniform. She laughed about that, too."

"Uniform?"

"That's all. Not what kind it was."

Runyon asked, "The first time she saw him at Stow Lake — what did he say to her?"

"He offered to buy her a soda. Erin said no, and that was the end of it."

"Did he tell her his name?"

"Well, he must have at some point, at least his first name."

"But she didn't mention it and you didn't ask."

"I didn't see any reason to."

"How soon did he turn up again after Stow Lake?"

"A few days later. At a tavern on Geary where she went sometimes."

"Talk to her there? Hit on her?"

"No, nothing like that. Just said hello and bought her a drink."

"And hung around, watched her?"

"In a worshipful way. He never bothered her."

"How many other times did she see him?"

"Once or twice more at the tavern. And once or twice when she was out jogging."

"Following her?"

"She didn't get that impression," Risa said. "She thought he might live in the neighborhood."

"Did he give her any idea where?"

"I don't think so."

"This went on, him turning up, for about a month?"

"No more than that. Then he must have lost interest or moved away."

"And your sister never saw him again?"

"I'm sure she'd have told me if she had." Risa paused before she said, "Two years is a long time."

Runyon said, "There aren't any time limits on sexual obsession."

"But why would he go away and then all of a sudden come back and attack her without provocation?"

"People disappear for any number of reasons. And there may have been provocation that night — a more aggressive approach, rejection, sudden rage and loss of control."

"My God."

"Just speculation at this point," Runyon said, "but worth looking into. What's the name of the tavern on Geary?"

"McRoyd's Irish Pub."

"And the name of the girlfriend who was with Erin at Stow Lake?"

"Sally Michaels. Sally Johnson now. She got married about six months ago and moved to Morgan Hill."

"Do you have an address and phone number?"

"Yes, but not here. At home."

"Call me on my cell phone when you get there. Number's on the card I gave you. All right?"

"All right. And . . . thank you, Jake."

Jake, not Mr. Runyon. With almost the same little catch in her voice Colleen had when she said his name —

No. Bullshit, Runyon. What's the matter with you?

He said gruffly, "There's nothing to thank me for yet," and broke the connection.

Nobody at McRoyd's Irish Pub knew a three-hundred-pound, ponytailed man or remembered anyone like that from more than a year ago. The bartender said, "Check back after six o'clock. The boss comes on then, Sam McRoyd. He's owned this place thirty years — he's got a memory like an elephant, knows just about everybody who ever lived around here."

"Thanks. I'll do that."

★ ★ ★

A woman's deep voice said, "Yes? This is Justine."

"Is your husband home, Mrs. Linden?"

"No, he isn't." Then, suspiciously, "Who is this?"

"My name is Runyon, I spoke to him this afternoon —"

"I know, he told me." Cold now, as if her voice had been quick-frozen in dry ice. "You should have come to me instead of Ralph."

"Would it have made a difference?"

"It might have. I'm not as easy to intimidate as he is."

"There was no intimidation. We had a conversation, that's all."

"You threatened him."

"Wrong. I don't make threats. He offered cooperation and I accepted, that's all."

Humming silence for several seconds. Then, "I suppose that's why you're calling. You want the key."

"If you're willing to put it in your mailbox and leave it there for the next couple of days, then you won't have to deal with me in person."

"And then what? You keep calling up and coming back whenever you feel like it?"

"Chances are you'll never hear from me again."

"What does that mean, 'chances are'?"

"Just what I said."

"How do I know you won't keep hassling us?"

"I'm not hassling you now," Runyon said. "I'm accepting your husband's offer. Unless you'd rather rescind it."

"Oh, sure. And then you'd go straight to the Housing Authority."

"No, I wouldn't do that."

"So you say."

"You have my word on it."

"Your word. How do I know you'd keep it?"

"You don't. You'll have to trust me, either way."

Heavy sigh, exaggerated. "You'd better not do any damage to our property."

"You don't have to worry about that."

"And if Mr. Troxell finds out you were snooping around, I won't take any abuse from him. I'll lay it all on your head."

"Or about that."

"The key will be in the goddamn mailbox," she said, and broke the connection.

13

Risa Niland

The past two months had been hard, so hard. She couldn't have gotten through them without the support from Mom and Dad, friends, neighbors, the people she worked with, and the customers at Get Fit. She'd've broken down completely and ended up in a hospital or institution. As it was she'd barely survived the first couple of weeks. Sleepless nights, depression, sudden crying fits. Nothing she tried, not Ambien or pot or vodka, made her days and nights any easier.

Time had accomplished that, finally. Some days now, for short periods, she was able to function more or less normally, without feeling the grief and anger and bitterness, without thinking of Erin at all. But other days were bad, like the ones in the first weeks — Erin in her mind almost every minute at the apartment, the health club, anywhere she happened to be. Scores of little reminders, constant flood of memories. Erin's room with her unmade bed and her clothing and cosmetics strewn every which way and Mr. Floppy, that grungy one-eyed stuffed dog she'd had since she was six, propped on its tail on her dresser; Erin laughing, Erin grumbling, Erin tipsy, Erin fresh from the shower and prancing nude around the apartment, Erin in all her moods from loving and generous when she got her way to spiteful and bitchy when she didn't. The time when she was twelve and they'd had their first long talk about sex, and the night when she was fifteen and she'd done it for the first time and was so excited and scared and couldn't wait to share all the gory details. The weird fun summer they'd spent on little Nicolet Island off the Wisconsin mainland. The whitewater rafting trip on the upper Colorado River three years ago with Jerry and that friend of his Erin called Needle Dick behind his back. So many things . . .

Today had been different from any of the others. Strange. Good and bad, both. Good because of that detective, Runyon, and his offer to help, and the reborn hope that someday there might be justice after all. Bad because the hope was so small, and because of the other man at the cemetery, not knowing who he was or why he'd bought the headstone and sent all the flowers. And because it seemed that everybody she came in contact with had also lost Erin or somebody else close to them. Each in turn made her feel her loss that much more intensely.

The headstone man, the flower man. If he wasn't the guilty one, then whoever he was and whatever the relationship he'd had with Erin, she must have been very important to him. And that meant he'd lost her, too.

Jake Runyon. Widower for ten months, his wife a victim of cancer. That must be just as terrible as losing a sister to sudden brutal violence. God, she'd looked into his eyes and it had been just like looking into her own in the mirror — all the suffering, all the sorrow, right there on the surface.

Scott. He'd really loved Erin, she hadn't realized how much until she saw how torn up he was. Erin had loved him, too, the first guy she'd ever been serious about. They'd probably have gotten married eventually, had kids despite Erin's hollow "no squalling brats for me" disclaimer. Had a good life together, a normal, uneventful, mostly happy life. A life that never would be.

Kate. Only three months since Noreen walked out on her after nine years, no warning, just announced one morning she was leaving. Losing a lover that way was a kind of death, too, and for a while it hurt almost as much. She knew that kind of loss, too, because she'd gone through it herself when she and Jerry split up. Kate was her friend as well as her boss, but she still had days when she was depressed and hard to deal with and this had been one of them.

Dave. Like Scott, he'd lost a woman he loved deeply — some kind of accident he couldn't talk about beyond hinting he was the cause of it. Came to the club two or three times a week and worked out on the machines for hours until he was exhausted. So quiet and sad, hardly talked to anyone but her. Broken birds of a feather. He'd been in such pain today, his buff body radiating it even from a distance, that she couldn't stand to be near him.

And Jerry. She was his loss, as he was hers, thirteen months ago. The blame was all his, one hundred percent — just couldn't keep that thing of his zipped up in his pants. Called again this afternoon, second call this week, about the twentieth since the funeral. He wanted her back, he'd come right out and said so — lousy timing as usual. So sorry, Risa, I never stopped loving you, Jana was a stupid mistake, I swear I'll never do it again, just give me another chance and I'll be there for you from now on, yada yada

yada. She still loved him at some level, she supposed, no use lying to herself about that; if all the love was gone she wouldn't have kept his name. But how could she trust him again? For God's sake, he'd even hit on Erin a couple of times, practically drooled on himself the day he showed up at the apartment without calling and she walked out of the bathroom naked. He swore the hits weren't serious, he was just joking around, but that didn't mean he wouldn't have screwed her or tried to screw her if she'd shown him any encouragement. No. They were divorced and they were going to stay divorced; he'd lost her and she'd lost him. One more loss that couldn't be undone, ever.

Long, strange, good-bad day. She was relieved when her shift ended and she could leave the club and escape home. The emptiness, all the reminders of Erin, made the apartment claustrophobic sometimes, but tonight it was preferable to facing all those other hurt and damaged lives.

Her building was only a dozen blocks from Get Fit; she'd been fortunate to find a job with such an easy commute. She seldom drove to work, usually either walked or took the 38 Geary bus depending on the weather and how tired she was. Tonight, despite an early blowing fog, she walked. Lost inside herself and paying only minimal attention to her surroundings, yet without really thinking about Erin or anything else: bolstering herself against the night ahead with exercise and the few minutes of freedom.

The apartment was more good-bad: a sanctuary, but a cold, empty one. She really ought to move to a new place. Or at least clean out Erin's room, keep a few mementos and send the rest of her things to Mom and Dad or give them to Goodwill. People kept advising her to do one or the other, and she knew they were right, but she just couldn't face either chore. No use kidding herself — it probably would be a long time before she could.

She poured herself a vodka and lime juice, and took it with her into the bathroom. The drink and a hot shower helped a little. Dressed again, she looked up Sally and Kevin Johnson's phone number in her computer address book and then called it, thinking that if Sally knew anything about Fatso that she didn't, it would be easier for her to get the information. But all she got was their machine. She decided against leaving a message, tapped out Runyon's cell phone number instead.

He had an odd sort of voice, gruff and

gentle at the same time, but without much inflection. This morning, the whole time he'd talked to her at the cemetery, he'd worn a sort of neutral expression, what Jerry called a poker face, so you couldn't be sure of what he was thinking behind those pained eyes. She wondered again, talking to him now, what kind of man he was. Honest and caring, she was pretty sure of that much. And if he had the usual male ideas he kept them under control — she'd believed him when he told her he didn't expect anything in return for his help. But aside from that, who was he deep inside? Her interest was both personal, because of Erin, and impersonal. Or maybe detached was a better word. Acts of kindness were few and far between these days. A man like Jake Runyon almost made her believe again that most people were good and God was good and the world wasn't always a rotten, ugly place. Almost.

When she told him she'd tried to call Sally, he said, "You think she might not talk to me?"

"No, I don't see why she wouldn't. I just wanted to save you some time and effort."

"Thanks, but there's no need. I know what questions to ask."

"Whatever you say."

"Thing is," he said, "this isn't much of a lead yet. I don't want you to get your hopes up prematurely."

"That won't happen," Risa said.

"All right. Have you remembered anything else about this man Fatso, anything that might help identify him?"

"No. It was a long time ago, and it just didn't seem important then. To Erin or to me."

"Well, if you do . . ."

"Yes, I'll let you know right away."

He said he would be in touch and broke the connection.

But he wouldn't have anything to tell her when she heard from him, she thought fatalistically. How could Erin's murderer be a man she'd hardly known two years ago and who'd done nothing more menacing than show up at McRoyd's a couple of times while she was there? It had to be a total stranger, some faceless psycho who'd picked her at random. He might be caught one day for some other crime, in two or five or ten or twenty years, and a DNA test would link him to Erin's murder and he'd confess or not confess, and then it would be over. Or he might never be caught and then it would never be over.

Grabbing at straws. That was all Jake

Runyon was doing. Like everybody else, herself included, just grabbing at straws.

Get her hopes up? God, no, that wouldn't happen, not now and maybe never again.

The phone rang ten minutes later, while she was mixing a second vodka and lime juice. Mom and Dad calling from Green Bay. Two more sufferers to round out the day. She told them about Runyon and what he was doing, downplaying it, but it lifted their spirits much more than it had hers. They were unshaken believers; they'd kept the faith all along. So had she, for a while, but her belief wasn't rock solid anymore. The more time that passed without some kind of resolution, the more it would crumble until there was nothing left.

They talked for twenty minutes, mostly about Erin even though she kept trying to steer the conversation to more mundane subjects. And the conversation left her feeling depressed. She put on a hip-hop CD, cheerful music that didn't cheer her any. She thought she ought to eat something, and made herself a third drink instead. That had better be the last; she was feeling them already, and if she drank any more she'd have a hangover tomorrow, and she hated hangovers. She wished she had some pot. Then she could really get stoned without worrying about how she'd feel in the morning.

Good-bad day turning into another bad night.

She wondered, sipping vodka, how long it would be before she had a good day, a good night. Really *good,* the kind where everything you did or heard or saw gave you pleasure and you were so happy and content you smiled and laughed for no reason at all.

She wondered, sipping vodka, if she would ever have that kind of day and night again.

14

Troxell left his house alone shortly past seven Thursday evening. Destination: Wisconsin Street, Potrero Hill. I camped at the curb three doors uphill from the Lindens' Stick Victorian and watched him leave his BMW empty-handed and head down the path alongside.

Then I sat in the cold, dark car and fretted about Kerry.

You live with someone long enough, you develop a finely calibrated sensor where the other person is concerned. It doesn't take long for the bells and whistles to go off when something isn't right. Little things, cumulative effect. The way she'd been acting lately, the brooding silences, the declining interest in intimacy. The unsatisfactory talk we'd had last night. The fact that she'd taken most of today off work without explanation at the office and without telling me; I'd found that out from her secretary. The fact that she hadn't been home at six thirty tonight. She must have come home and then gone out again somewhere with Emily; nobody had answered my call to the condo and both their cell phones were out of service, which probably meant they were in a restaurant; we had strict rules about cells being turned off in public places. But why hadn't she let me know they were going so I wouldn't worry?

If the Dancer business was what was bothering her, I couldn't understand why she hadn't simply brought it out into the open. If it was something else . . . what? Some sort of medical problem? She'd had her annual physical a couple of weeks ago, but I'd asked her about it and she'd said everything was as it should be. Why would she tell me that if it wasn't?

Me? General dissatisfaction with our relationship, our life together? That notion scared hell out of me. We'd always been so good together, so completely in synch. Problems, sure, every marriage has some friction from time to time, but nothing serious, nothing that we hadn't managed to work out with a minimum of difficulty. She might be pissed at me for keeping secrets about Dancer and Cybil, but I couldn't conceive of her being angry enough to lose faith, start falling out of love —

Another man?

Well, it had happened . . . almost happened . . . once before. Paul Blessing, Blessing Furniture Showrooms, one of Bates and Carpenter's clients. But that had been before we were married, and it hadn't amounted to much. Strong physical attraction, a few dates, that was all. She hadn't gone to bed with him. Said she hadn't, and I'd believed her — I still believed her. No, it wasn't another man. She wouldn't cheat on me any more than I would cheat on her.

What, then?

Round and round . . .

I'd figured I was in for another of those long, dull, butt-cramping waits, while Troxell took his time doing whatever he did in his private hideaway, but it didn't turn out that way. He spent less than an hour in there tonight. When he reappeared he had something tucked under one arm, not too bulky; I could make out a faint gleam of white when he opened the driver's door on the BMW and the inside light came on. Plastic sack? Might be rental videos, viewed and ready for return, but I couldn't be sure at the distance.

Down off Potrero Hill, south on 101, west on 280. But he wasn't going home yet. He stayed on 280 until the Daly City interchange, swung off on John Daly Boulevard and from there onto Skyline north, past Fort Funston and Lake Merced. Heading for the beach? Right. He took the cutoff onto the Great Highway, then turned into the narrow beachfront parking area at the foot of Sloat Boulevard. I drove on past, circled the block onto Sloat, and crossed into the parking area from there.

The BMW was dark, slotted about halfway down. I pulled up between it and one other car parked there, close enough to the BMW for my headlights to wash over it and let me see that it was empty. I shut off the lights and got out and went to where I could see down beyond a shelf of broken shingle to the beach.

Broken clouds tonight, restless and shifting under the lash of a stiff, cold wind that had driven the temperature down into the low forties. The three-quarters moon was obscured at first, the beach like an expanse of black velvet except for the trim of faint luminescence where the surf broke and creamed over the sand. I stayed put, braced and shivering, until the moon broke free and I had a clearer view. One man down there, moving in hunched walk toward the waterline. Troxell, who else? Anybody's guess what quirk or impulse or demon sent him beach-walking at night, in frigid weather like this.

Back in the car, I sat on my hands until they warmed up and then called Jake Runyon's cell phone number. "Troxell went up to Potrero Hill again, but he didn't stay long. He's back at the beach now, taking a moonlight stroll."

"Going home from there, you think?"

"Probably."

"Be a good time for me to use that key."

"Yeah."

"Worth the risk. My opinion."

I hesitated, but not too long, before I said, "If you're game, I suppose I am, too. You won't take anything, disturb anything?"

"You know I won't."

"Sure. Worry mode tonight."

"Go ahead then?"

"Go. Let me know when you're finished."

I sat fidgeting, paying too much attention to the time, thinking that I ought to call home again and telling myself to quit worrying for no good reason. Eight thirty wasn't late; if Kerry and Emily weren't home by ten or eleven, that was the time to start fingering the panic button.

Less than half an hour dribbled away before Troxell trudged back to his car. Too cold on the beach tonight even for him. Go

160

home now, brother, I thought, when he headed out of the lot.

And that was what he did.

They were at the condo when I got there, both of them. Relief didn't hang around long; as soon as I knew they were safe, it gave way to a simmer of other emotions, one of them being low-grade anger. I had a headache, I was hungry, I wanted a beer and some aspirin and some food and some explanations. I got all of that, more or less, but none of it made me feel any better.

Kerry was sitting in her recliner in the living room, in the dark, alone except for Shameless curled up in her lap, the drapes open over the picture window and the lights of the city shining hard and bright in the distance. Emily was in her room with the door shut; I could see the light under the door. I called out to Kerry, got a lackluster response, and detoured into the kitchen. No dinner waiting, hot or cold. So I washed down three aspirin with a long draught from a bottle of Sierra Nevada, ate a cold chicken leg and a couple of carrots out of the refrigerator. Elegant dining in the bosom of home. Then, bottle in hand, I went into the living room to have a little fireside chat with my mate.

As far as I could tell she hadn't shifted position. When I switched on one of the table lamps I saw that she was sitting half-slouched, a sloppy posture she almost never adopts, and that she had a glass of white wine in one hand. She glanced up, favored me with a skeletal smile, and refocused her attention on the city lights below.

I said, "So?"

"So what?"

"You haven't been home long. Where were you tonight?"

"Emily and I went out to dinner."

"Uh-huh. How come I didn't get invited?"

"It wasn't planned. I didn't get home until after six and I didn't feel like cooking."

"I have a cell phone now. You gave it me last Christmas, remember?"

"You said you'd be working tonight. I didn't want to bother you."

"I was a lot more bothered not hearing from you."

"Well, I'm sorry. I should have called."

"Yes, you should have. How was work today?"

"Work?"

"You know, the daily grind at the city's leading ad agency."

"I took most of the day off," she said.

"I know. I called your office before I left the agency."

She glanced at me again, but only briefly; the city lights and the contents of her wineglass seemed to hold more appeal for her than I did. I sat down in my chair. The cat opened one eye for the first time, closed it again almost immediately. He wasn't interested in me tonight, either.

"I had a lunch date with Cybil," she said.

"Must've been some marathon lunch."

"And some things to do afterward."

"Such as?"

"Things," she said. "Are you interrogating me?"

"I'd have to suspect you of something for it to be an interrogation."

"Do you suspect me of something?"

"Nope. I'm just making conversation. Or trying to."

Silent communion with her wineglass.

"How's Cybil?" I asked her.

"All right."

"What did the two of you talk about?"

"What do you think we talked about?"

That pushed the wrong button, turned up the heat under my frustration. "Kerry, dammit, what's the matter with you? Talk to me. Please."

Some time went by. She still wasn't

looking at me. Shameless got up, stretched, yawned, turned around twice and settled down again with a little trilling sigh.

Kerry matched the sigh. "I'm not angry with you, you know."

"Angry with *me?*"

"I ought to be, but I'm not. With you or with Cybil."

"Oh, Christ. So that's it."

"I understand the two of you were only trying to protect me, but I have the right to know the truth. More right than anybody in this world. More reason, too."

"Cybil told you, then. All of it?"

"All of it. I dragged it out of her at lunch."

"How long have you suspected?"

"Since Dancer died. Even before that. Something about the way the two of them interacted the few times I saw them together, as if there was a secret between them . . . it always made me uneasy."

"You never said anything —"

"We don't tell each other everything. No matter how much we pretend otherwise."

"Kerry, I'm sorry. I promised Cybil —"

"I know. I also know you figured it out and confronted her with it. Would you have told me if you hadn't promised?"

". . . I'm not sure. I hate keeping secrets, but I didn't want to hurt you without reason. Keeping quiet seemed the lesser of the two evils."

Two swallows of wine before she said, "Without reason? Dancer's child, rape child."

"No. He wasn't your father, Ivan was. Cybil's convinced of that."

"But I'm not. Not as long as there's even the remotest chance."

"What are you going to do?"

"Have a DNA test done. Cybil has a lock of Ivan's hair."

"It's that important to you to know for sure?"

"Yes. It's that important."

"Why now, all of a sudden?"

"What do you mean, all of a sudden?"

"It's been three months since Dancer died. If you suspected then, why didn't you say something? Why wait so long to get it out into the open?"

"You're interrogating me again," she said.

"I'm not. I'm only —"

"Denial, all right? It took me a long time to face up to it, make up my mind."

Logical answer, but I had the feeling it was only a half-truth, an evasion. She wasn't looking at me when she gave it, and there was a flat, defensive quality in her voice. Her face, lamplit in profile, seemed tight-set, little white ridges of muscle showing around her mouth.

I said, "When are you going to have the test done?"

"Right away. I've already made arrangements."

"Well, that's good. The sooner it's done, the sooner we can all get past this."

"If Ivan's DNA is a match with mine."

"It will be."

"We'll see."

"All right, suppose it isn't. What then?"

"I'll deal with it," she said.

"Would it change how you feel about your life, yourself?"

"I said I'd deal with it." Snappish now. "One way or another."

An uncomfortable little silence built between us. I could feel the tension radiating out of her; it was strong enough to prickle the hairs on my neck. The cat felt it, too. He got up, gave her a sideways look, made a noise in his throat, and jumped down.

"Kerry," I said, "what is it you're not telling me?"

Her head turned briefly, turned away again.

"You're holding something back, hiding something."

"Like you did the past three months?"

"Punishing me, is that it?"

"No. Don't be silly."

"All right, then. Why? What is it?"

No answer.

"Is there some other reason you're in a rush for that DNA test?"

No answer.

"Kerry, please, no more secrets. Just talk to me."

She looked at me again, locked her gaze onto mine. Slowly her face lost some of its tautness, and her eyes softened and she wet her lips and started to say something —

And my goddamn cell phone went off.

The thing was in my coat pocket, but it had one of those chirpy rings that seem overloud even when muffled. It startled both of us; worse, it changed Kerry's mind, closed her off again. In the time it took for a second loud chirp, the muscles in her face retightened and her attention shifted back to the city lights.

"You'd better answer that," she said.

"It's probably Jake Runyon, he'll call back. Kerry —"

"I think I'll have another glass of wine," she said, and got abruptly to her feet and walked out of the room. I knew that walk, the stubborn set of her head and shoulders.

No matter what I said or did, I would not get anything more out of her until she was good and ready to give it to me.

15

Jake Runyon

The key was in the Lindens' mailbox, attached by a chain and hook to a hunk of var-
nished driftwood. Justine Linden's doing,
probably. Afraid of it being lost, or maybe
the driftwood was a feeble attempt to annoy
him. He wasn't annoyed; there were too
many large concerns for him to be bothered
by the pettiness in people.

He came down off the front stoop, went
around onto the path at the side. The key
opened the gate lock as well. There were
lights showing at the front of the house, but
none back here. All the windows looked to
be blinded or draped. Throbbing music,
something jazzy with heavy emphasis on
saxophone and trumpet, came from inside
— loud out here, which meant it must be
deafening inside. They didn't want to know
if and when he came prowling around. The
old, false credo: what you don't know can't
hurt you.

The outbuilding was dark except for a re-
flected gleam where moonlight touched

window glass. Runyon crossed the patch of damp grass to the entrance. The key let him into shadows and silence, and the faint musty smell of a place that hadn't been aired out in some time. He shut the door behind him before he felt around for a wall switch.

The switch operated a pair of lamps set well apart from each other, both with low-wattage bulbs which allowed his eyes to adjust immediately to the light. One big room, with a fake knotty pine partition that separated a third of it into a bedroom area, and a closed door at that end that would lead to the bathroom. The other two-thirds was a combination living room and kitchenette, no separation between them. Single-beam ceiling covered with white acoustical tile, walls paneled in more fake knotty pine. Pretty rudimentary. Justine Linden and her brother must not have thought much of their mother. Either that, or they'd built the unit on the cheap out of necessity or parsimony.

Carpeted floor, threadbare in places. Not much in the way of furnishings: sofa, Naugahyde chair, coffee table, end table, TV and VCR on a rolling stand, day bed, dresser, two-burner stove top, tiny refrigerator, stainless-steel sink set into a narrow

Formica countertop. No visible phone. Light film of dust on the furniture, and that musty smell: Troxell hadn't bothered to clean the place. But he hadn't messed it up any, either. There was nothing on any of the tables or countertop. The only evidence of his occupation were two medium-sized cardboard boxes on the floor next to the couch, a tall pile of newspapers beside the coffee table, and a pair of video cassettes on top of the VCR.

Runyon went around the partition into the bedroom area. The day bed was unmade, no sheets or blankets anywhere. A tiny closet contained dust bunnies and empty hangers. The dresser drawers were empty. Nothing in the bathroom except a bar of soap on a tray that hadn't been used in so long it had turned stone-hard and developed cracks. He crossed to the other end and opened the re-frigerator. Empty. Under the sink was a wastebasket; nothing in there, either.

One of the videos was a slasher film called *Bloodbath*, the usual crap about a psychotic slaughtering young women. The other was a graphic reality thing in a plain box with a typed title — *True Terror: The Most Hor-rifying Deaths Ever Captured on Film.* Touching it made Runyon want to go wash his hands.

He moved over to the cartons. The largest one contained some twenty books, hardcovers and paperbacks both, some with library markings, some new. Serial killer novels. Accounts of high-profile true-crime cases, all involving violent homicide. A sociological study titled *The Effects of Violence in American Society*, another on the causes and consequences of domestic abuse called *Look What You Made Me Do*. Abnormal psychology texts: *The Killing Mind*, *Why Did They Kill?*, *The Psychopathology of Rape*, *Monsters in Disguise: An Illustrated History of Serial Killers.*

He repacked the books in the order he'd found them, opened the second carton. Manila file folders, more than a dozen of them, each with a woman's name printed on the front with a black felt-tip pen. One of the names was Erin Dumont; he recognized three of the others as violent-crime victims whose funerals Troxell had attended. All the names, he found, belonged to victims of either random or domestic violence. Each folder contained a sheaf of newspaper clippings detailing the circumstances of the crime, follow-up news and feature stories, resolution if any; and receipts for floral and memorial offerings. There were four times the number of receipts in the Dumont folder as in any of the others — for flowers sent once or twice weekly, the marble headstone, an annual upkeep payment on her grave. That was all. No notations in Troxell's hand, no additional contents of any kind.

Two other items in the box. One was a thick bunch of nonreligious Hallmark cards bound together by a rubber band. All new and of more or less the same design, with simple messages: deepest sympathy, heartfelt condolences. Ready to be signed with something anonymous like "A Friend" and sent to victims' families with or without floral offerings.

The final item in the box was the most interesting of the lot. Pad of ruled yellow foolscap, new, with none of the sheets having been torn off. Five pages had writing on them, all of it in Troxell's crabbed hand. The top sheet had been done with a ballpoint, the penmanship good and the rows orderly until the last few sentences; those sentences sprawled and had been written with enough pressure to tear the paper in a few places. Rough draft of a letter that had never been sent:

To the S.F. Police Department —
Three nights ago, at approximately

7 p.m., I was at Lloyd Lake in Golden Gate Park. I stop there sometimes on my way home from work, sit at Portals of the Past and watch the ducks, it's a quiet place to unwind.

I was returning to my car when I noticed a man and a woman talking alongside a car parked across the road from mine. There was no one else in the vicinity. The man was holding the door open. The woman hesitated as if she was reluctant to get inside, then relented. The man got in after her. I don't believe either of them noticed me.

He didn't start the car or put on the lights. As I was buckling my seat belt, I saw them talking and the woman began to laugh. It seemed to make him angry. He said something to her and she stopped laughing. She tried to get out of the car. He grabbed her, dragged her back. I think he might have hit her then. No, I'm sure he did, he punched her in the face, the dome light was on and I saw her head bounce off the door glass and her body slump down on the seat. He pulled the door shut. He started the car and drove away.

I could have followed them but I didn't.

I sat there a while longer and then I drove home.

I didn't do anything.

It was dark and I didn't get a clear look at the woman but she was young and she was wearing a light-colored jogging suit. I think she might be the woman who was raped and murdered that night.

I can't identify the man, I didn't get a clear look at him.

I can't identify the make or model of the car.

I couldn't read the license plate number.

I don't really know anything.

I didn't do anything.

I can't I couldn't I don't I didn't

The other four pages had been written with a black felt-tip pen. Some of it was the same crabbed handwriting as the letter draft, some was in block printing, a few words had been formed in thick, heavy, doodlelike strokes. Done at different times, but in each case during a period of emotional upheaval.

The first:

american? japanese?
2 doors 4 doors?
dark color but what color? dark blue

175

dark green dark brown?
   license plate? 2 something U or O or D
but that's all
   big man but just husky or fat?
   what kind of cap? baseball racing sun
what?
   don't know can't remember couldn't
tell in the dark
   didnt pay enough attention
   why not?
   you coward you know why not

The second:

   cant
   cant
   coward
   cant
   coward
   coward
   coward

The third:

   why why why why whywhywhywhy-
whywhywhywhywhy
   WHY
   WHY!!!!!

The last:

cant stop any of it from happening
cant understand it
cant get away from it
in the midst of life we are in death
its all around us everywhere

SO

MUCH

DEATH

Runyon used the small digital camera he carried to photograph each of the five sheets. Then he replaced the pad, closed the carton. There was nothing else to see in the studio; he'd seen enough, more than enough.

He went back out into the cold night.

"Christ," Bill said, "I was afraid of something like that."

"Better to know than not. For everybody."

"Except us. Evidence obtained by illegal trespass. We can't sit on it, and that puts us smack between a rock and a hard place."

"I'll take responsibility if it comes to that. You didn't order me to get the key."

"I didn't order you not to, either."

"How do you want to handle it?"

"I don't know yet. I'll need to sleep on it, take a look at those digitals, talk to Tamara.

One thing for sure: We're off this case, as of right now."

Runyon didn't argue. He put his cell away, started the car. The Troxell surveillance might be finished, but not the Erin Dumont homicide investigation. Not for Risa Niland. And not for him.

Still nobody home at the Johnson number in Morgan Hill.

McRoyd's Irish Pub was noisy and crowded, standing-room only at the bar, two bartenders on duty and both needed. The older of the barkeeps was Sam Mc-Royd, a bantam of a man in his sixties, white-haired, garrulous — a court-holder who spent as much time arguing and bantering with his customers as he did mixing drinks. It took Runyon ten minutes to claim a stool, another fifteen minutes to get McRoyd's ear and ask his questions.

"Weighed three hundred pounds, ye say? Wore his hair in one of them ponytails?"

"That's right."

"And a uniform?"

"Might have worn one in here, might not."

"Don't place him. Not a regular customer. Let me think on it a minute."

Runyon ordered a draft beer. McRoyd

went to draw it, and when he came back he said, "Now I recall the lad. Giants fan. Steroids."

"Steroids?"

"Didn't see nothing wrong with players like Barry Bonds using 'em. Winning was all that mattered to him, never mind fair play. We had a few sharp words about that nonsense, one night."

"What else can you tell me about him?"

"Drank Guinness. The right way, slow, to savor the taste. Quiet except for his Giants fever and his crap about steroids. Wore a Giants cap. Turned around with the bill in back, like a catcher before he puts on his mask."

"Every time he was here?"

"Seems like. Never took it off."

"But no uniform?"

"No uniform," McRoyd said.

"Did he talk to anybody besides you? Another customer?"

"Not that I recall."

"Give you any idea where he lived or worked?"

"Baseball, that's the sum of it."

Runyon took a little more than that away with him. Giants fan, Giants cap, didn't wear a uniform after working hours. Not much, but something.

big man but just husky or fat?

what kind of cap? baseball racing sun what?

And maybe more than just a little something.

In his cold apartment he brewed a cup of tea and then downloaded the five digital photos onto his laptop. They were all good shots, the writing clearly readable in each. He created and saved a file for them, e-mailed the file to Tamara's computer at the agency.

He carried his cup into the bedroom, sat on the bed and looked at the silver-framed portrait of Colleen on the nightstand. Her smiling image held his attention for a long time, until the tea was gone and his eyes began to ache and his vision to swim a little at the edges. Then he got up, returned to the living room, switched on the TV for noise. Sat staring at the screen without seeing it.

There was a tight strain of anger in him now. Troxell. The world at large. But mainly it was for himself, for letting the loneliness and the grief get to him again and because he still couldn't get Risa Niland out of his mind.

16

Lynn Troxell wasn't alone when I showed up at her home for our late Friday morning appointment. I wouldn't have minded if her other visitor was Charles Kayabalian. I wanted to talk to him, in fact had tried to arrange a joint meeting with the two of them, but he was tied up and unavailable until later in the day. A one-on-one conference with Mrs. Troxell was the next best choice. I wasn't prepared for or comfortable with a one-on-two with her and Drew Casement.

The way she looked didn't help the situation much, either. Dressed in a black pants suit and a dark blue blouse, no color anywhere, her face pale without makeup, her expression bleak and that quality of deep sadness more pronounced. Expecting the worst and put together accordingly. Another mourner.

She greeted me gravely, as a widow might, and ushered me through a formal living room filled with the kind of antique furniture nobody ever sits on, into a large and more comfortable family room with a row of windows overlooking a rear garden. And there was Casement, on his feet and wearing an expression to match hers. At least he didn't look like he was on his way to a funeral: light blue golf shirt and beige slacks, the picture of health with that tanned skin and rugged manner.

I couldn't keep a frown off my face when I saw him. He said, "Lynn said it's okay for me to be here. I'm just as worried about Jim as she is."

She said, "Please, it's all right. I want Drew to stay."

It wasn't worth arguing about. "Whatever you say, Mrs. Troxell."

She did the hostess thing, offering coffee or something else to drink, and I declined, and we all got settled in a little half-circle, her on a rose-patterned sofa and Casement and me on chairs. Out in the garden there were pale sunshine and noisy birds working around a pedestal feeder, but in here it was hushed and darker than it should have been despite all the light outside. Too much melancholy on my mind, maybe, but the atmosphere was such that I wouldn't have been surprised to hear sepulchral music playing soft and low in the background.

Nobody said anything as I opened my

briefcase and took out the report Tamara had prepared. She and Runyon and I had held a conference earlier, after I looked at the digital photos he'd taken, and we'd agreed on the only viable course open to us if we wanted to avoid potential repercussions. So the report was a slightly doctored account of our investigation — accurate except for any mention of Runyon's illegal trespass last night and details on what he'd found in the rental unit. The Erin Dumont case was a focal point, but presented in allusions and inferences couched in general terms — "confidential sources indicate" and "we have good reason to believe." None of us liked doing it this way, but we liked the prospect of heavy legal expenses and possible license suspensions a hell of a lot less. Sometimes you have to bend the rules a little to get at the truth, and when you do that, sometimes you have to bend them a little more for maintenance reasons. It's that kind of business; it's that kind of cover-your-ass world.

Immediately I handed the report to Mrs. Troxell, Casement got up and went to sit beside her on the sofa so he could read along with her. I looked out into the garden and watched the birds chattering at the feeder. When I shifted my gaze back to the two of them, Mrs. Troxell's face was the color of buttermilk and Casement had his arm around her shoulders. The only change in his expression was a tightening of the muscles bracketing his mouth.

She finished reading the last page, sat so rigidly she seemed almost to have stopped breathing. It was nearly half a minute before she moved, a sudden spasmodic lifting of head and breast. "God," she said, "all of this . . . I can't . . ." She could not seem to articulate the rest of what she was thinking, shook her head and fell silent.

Casement said grimly, "Worse than we expected. A lot worse."

I didn't say anything.

"You sure about Jim seeing what happened in the park, not doing anything about it?"

"If we weren't, it wouldn't be in the report."

"So that's what set him off on all the rest of it — the trigger we were talking about yesterday. Guilt, not being able to face himself."

"Evidently."

"Christ. Funerals, cemeteries, a rented hideaway, night walks on the beach —"

Lynn Troxell found her voice. "Jim has always been drawn to water," she said distantly, not quite a non sequitur. "The ocean, lakes, rivers. They have a calming effect on him."

Casement said, "He needs more than water. Prozac or Ritalin, maybe."

"I suppose so, but . . ." She shuddered and looked at me. "I don't understand about the granny unit. What does he do there?"

What does he do? I thought. He wallows in death, that's what he does. But I said, "What he can't do here because he's afraid you'll find out and he wants to spare you." And spare himself at the same time.

"Reads newspapers looking for violent crimes," Casement said, "so he can attend the victims' funerals. Broods. Christ knows what else."

"How can he be that obsessed, that . . . sick and I didn't have any idea of it?"

"Don't go blaming yourself, Lynn. He's so closed off, nobody could've known how bad he is."

"I should have," she insisted. "I knew about the murders he saw as a child, I should have realized . . ."

Casement tightened his grip on her shoulder. He said to me, "The other thing we talked about yesterday . . . you think he could be building up to suicide?"

I gave him a sharp warning look.

185

"No, it's all right, Lynn and I talked about that, too. I told you, we don't have any secrets."

She said, "I can't imagine Jim doing a thing like that. I just . . . can't."

"I can," Casement said, "and I wish I couldn't. What he said to me that day, the look on his face — he's capable of it, all right."

"What are we going to do?" Then, desperately: "We have to do something!"

"Talk to him," I said, "convince him to get professional help."

"A psychiatrist?"

"He wouldn't agree to it," Casement said.

"He might. What other choice do we have?"

I said, "Frankly, none that I can see."

She blinked, frowned, pulled her shoulders back the way people do when a sudden thought strikes them. She asked me, "The police . . . you haven't told them about Jim being a witness?"

"Not yet."

"Do you have to?"

"I'm obligated to. Withholding information in a homicide case is a felony, no matter who does it or what the reason."

"When? How soon?"

The correct answer to that was immediately. The one mitigating factor in favor of a delay: two months had already passed since Erin Dumont's murder, and assuming that what Troxell had scrawled in his notes was the whole truth, he had no specific knowledge that could lead to identification and arrest of the perp. But then there was the unknown factor: his mental state. How close was he to acting on a suicidal impulse? No way to tell from outward appearances. Confronting him might shock him into facing his illness, force him to take action to help himself. It might also push him over the line into an act of self-destruction. For that matter, so might being detained as a material witness, having the truth about his cowardice come out that way. A risk in any case, and not my decision to make.

I said all of this to Lynn Troxell, adding, "I can give you a little time if you want it. The choice is yours."

"How much time?"

"Until Monday morning. Either your husband goes to the police voluntarily by then or I'll have to do it and then they'll come after him."

"I don't know . . . I don't know what's best."

Casement said, "We've got to talk to him, Lynn."

"I suppose so . . . yes."

I said, "Have Kayabalian — and your family physician — present when you do. Show him the report if you have to."

"Let Jim know I hired a detective to spy on him?"

"We'll make him understand you did it for his own good," Casement said.

Her long, graceful hands moved in her lap, lacing and interlacing in that nervously habitual way of hers. Anguish bent her features into disproportionate shapes, like a face in a Dali painting. Casement and I both watched her struggle with decision, the anguish finally settle into a dull determination that readjusted her features and reestablished her poise.

"You're right," she said, "there's no other way."

"You won't have to do it alone. I'll be right there with you."

She nodded and asked me, "Does Charles know about any of this yet?"

"No. I have a meeting scheduled with him later this afternoon. I'll brief him then."

"All right." Her voice and her manner were more forceful now. Making the decision seemed to have given her strength. "Please tell him to call me. I'll contact Jim's

188

doctor and explain the situation to him and we'll coordinate a time."

I said I would.

Casement patted her arm; she returned the pat, absently, and got to her feet. "How much do I owe you for your services?" she asked. "I'll give you a check before you leave."

I didn't blame her for that. Once the dirty work is done in cases like this, the professional advice dispensed and considered, the important questions asked and answered, the clients focus on the primary issues and the hired guns like me become superfluous; we're unpleasant reminders of the fact that we were necessary in the first place and they want us out of their lives as quickly as possible. One more reason you need a thick skin to be a detective.

Tamara had prepared a final invoice; I gave it to Mrs. Troxell, and she wrote out a check and offered her thanks in return. She wasn't really seeing me anymore, except peripherally, and Casement's attention was all on her. None of us bothered to shake hands or say good-bye. Even before I let myself out, I felt as though I'd dematerialized — a latter-day invisible man.

"How'd it go?" Tamara asked.

"About as we expected," I said. "I gave her a three-day grace period. And I'm not sure it wasn't a big mistake. Troxell is probably suicidal and the shock could trigger him the wrong way. I don't want that on my conscience."

"Her choice. You didn't make it for her."

"Still."

"She's not gonna do it alone?"

"No. With Kayabalian and their family doctor present. And Drew Casement. Casement was there with her this morning. She wanted him to sit in, let him read the report."

"Something wrong with that? He's a family friend, right?"

"He also happens to be in love with her."

"Yeah? How do you know?"

"Pretty obvious. The way he looks at her, acts around her."

"She feel the same way? Two of them getting it on together?"

"No, it's not like that. She may not even know how he feels. The only person she's in love with is her poor bastard of a husband."

"So why do you care how Casement feels about her?"

"I don't, really. Just an observation."

"Lots of people in love with people they

hadn't ought to be who don't love them back, you know what I'm saying?"

"True enough."

"Love," Tamara said with sudden vehemence. "Love is bullshit."

"Now what brought that on?"

Big breath. "Nothing. Like you said, just an observation."

"One I don't happen to agree with. Neither did you, not so long ago."

"Yeah, well."

"Things aren't good between you and Horace, are they? You can talk to me, you know —"

She said, "I've got work to do," and went scowling into her office and shut the connecting door.

Women and their secrets. Kerry, Cybil, Tamara. Emily, too, someday, no doubt. Then I thought: Come on, women don't have a monopoly on keeping things to themselves. James Troxell is living proof of that. Hell, so are you, you narrow-minded, moralistic jerk.

The meeting with Charles Kayabalian went all right. He asked a couple of questions about the source of our information, and I hedged by saying, "I'd rather not reveal that. We had to take risks to get it, in the best interests of all concerned." He's a smart man, Kayabalian; he guessed or had a pretty good idea of what the risks were. He said he'd rather not know anyway, since I wasn't his client and anything I told him would not be privileged, and we left it at that.

He said he'd let me know how the meeting with Troxell turned out; his grimace added that he wasn't looking forward to it and his expectations weren't high. Neither were mine, but it wasn't my problem any longer. I hoped.

By the time I ransomed my car from the nearest parking garage, it was after three thirty, and Friday afternoon commute traffic was already clogging the downtown streets. I had one more piece of business to attend to, but I didn't need to return to the agency to get it done. I headed home instead. It would be well after four when I got there, and the odds were good that Jack Logan would be off duty and I could leave a message on his voice mail: "Our investigation on that case I mentioned turned up a witness connection to the Erin Dumont homicide, Jack. We're in the process of trying to verify it. I'll lay it out for you Monday morning in any case."

More C.Y.A. manipulation. If Troxell

could be kept in one piece and persuaded to report to the Hall of Justice by Monday, the police wouldn't care how or why he'd been prodded into it. If he didn't, we'd be officially on record as cooperating.

17

Jake Runyon

He called the Morgan Hill number before nine Friday morning, and this time he got an answer. Male voice, young and suspicious when he asked for Sally Johnson. Even when he identified himself and stated his business, the suspicion remained.

"Detective? What the hell do you want with my wife? She doesn't know anything about any murder."

In the background a woman's voice said, "Kevin? Who is that?"

The husband said into the phone, "How do I know you're who you say you are anyway?"

"Would you like references?"

". . . You trying to be a wiseass?"

"Five minutes of your wife's time, that's all I'm asking."

"Why? I told you, she doesn't know any-thing —"

"Kevin, let me talk to the man. If he's calling about Erin, maybe I can help —"

"Yeah, right. Some fucking guy, he could

be anybody, one of your boyfriends for all I know —"

"Oh, for God's sake. Give me that phone!"

There was more, the exchange loud and angry but muffled by a hand clapped over the mouthpiece. Then the woman's voice, breathless and angry, said, "Yes, hello? This is Sally —" Sharp door-slamming sound in the background. "God, I don't know why I married him. He can be *such* an asshole!"

Runyon made no comment.

"You're a detective? Calling about Erin?"

"That's right. My name is Runyon."

"Oh God, I couldn't believe it when I heard what happened. She and I . . . we were really close . . . it makes me sick every time I think about it . . . but I don't know anything, I hadn't seen her for months before it happened, it must've been some crazy person . . ."

He told her why he was calling.

"Fatso?" she said. "Oh, sure, I remember him. But that was what, more than two years ago, and there was no hassle or anything. He was just this big sloppy fat guy. You don't think he — ?"

"Checking possibilities," Runyon said shortly. "You were with Erin at Stow Lake the first time she saw him?"

"Yes, right, Stow Lake. It was a Saturday,

we went up there to ride the paddle boats, you know, just goofing around. We were at the snack bar when he came up and said hello to Erin. I remember he looked at her the whole time, like I wasn't even there."

"Did he introduce himself, give his name?"

"Um, no, I don't think so. Not that day, and not the other time, either. The only other time I saw him, I mean."

"Where was that?"

"At this bar we used to go to, an Irish pub on Geary."

"McRoyd's?"

"Right, McRoyd's."

"How do you suppose he knew Erin hung out there?"

She thought that over. "I think maybe he overheard us talking about it at Stow. We'd been at the pub the night before, one of the guys was celebrating his birthday and got blasted and did a bare-ass strip . . . it was hilarious and we were laughing about it when Fatso came over."

"Any idea what kind of car he drove?"

"Fatso? No, all I ever saw him in was the delivery truck."

"Delivery truck?"

"At Stow. That's what he was doing there, making deliveries to the snack bar."

"What kind of deliveries?"

"I'm not sure, let me think. . . . No, I just don't remember."

"How about the truck? Big, medium, small?"

"Sort of medium, I guess."

"Open bed or closed shell?"

"Closed shell? You mean like a van?"

"Yes."

"I'm pretty sure that's what it was, a kind of medium-sized van."

"What color?"

"White."

"The same as his uniform?"

"That's right, that was white, too." Sally Johnson let loose a sudden small giggling sound. "Erin thought he looked like a fat shaggy dog, one of those English sheep dogs, you know? But to me . . . well, *I* thought he looked like the Pillsbury doughboy —"

Runyon had no more patience for that crap; he cut her off with a sharp question. "The type of uniform with the company name on the back?"

". . . I think maybe. But it was such a long time ago . . ."

"Painted on the side of the delivery van, too?"

"Um, yes."

"Close your eyes, think hard, try to picture it. The company name, the type of product."

He waited through close to a minute of humming silence before she said, "I'm sorry, I really am, but I just can't remember. . . ."

The weather was good today, mostly clear, and a number of citizens were taking advantage of it when Runyon arrived at Stow Lake. Joggers, a few paddle boaters and canoers, people wandering the paths, others seated on benches and strips of grass reading, taking in the sun, watching the ducks and seabirds floating on the dirty brown water.

He followed the loop road to the parking area behind the boathouse at the western end. He'd been here once before, as he'd been to a great many locales in the city and the surrounding communites since his move down from Seattle — cataloging his new territory so he could move around freely without having to look at a map and he'd know what to expect from each place if and when his work took him there. Stow Lake was man-made, built around the base of Strawberry Hill, a four-hundred-foot wooded elevation turned into an island centerpiece accessible by a pair of pedestrian bridges. A network of paths and the boathouse and dock on this side, more paths, a waterfall, even a Chinese pagoda on the islet. Colleen would have liked it here. Quiet, nice scenery, good spot for a picnic.

He went around to the combination snack bar and boat-rental counter. Two kids on duty, one selling hot dogs, sodas, ice cream, the other handling the rentals. Neither had an answer to his questions; the longest either of them had been working there was eleven months, and no, none of the deliverymen they knew weighed three hundred pounds and wore their hair in ponytails. White uniforms? Sure, lots of delivery guys wore uniforms, they just never paid much attention.

The double doors to the repair and maintenance shop adjacent were open. Runyon spent two minutes with the man on duty, and came out again with nothing more than he'd gone in with. He stood for a time scanning the bench-sitters in the vicinity. Two possibilities, one man and one woman, both older than sixty and with the relaxed look and posture of regulars. The woman had nothing to tell him. He moved on to where the man sat at the end of the dock area, near the small flotilla of canoes and multicolored paddle boats.

White-haired, heavily lined face, seventy or more. He lifted his head when Runyon sat down next to him, peered through thick-lensed glasses. Mildly annoyed at first at being disturbed, but he was the naturally gregarious type and he showed interest when Runyon identified himself and asked his questions.

"Yep. Weather permits, I'm usually here." His voice was clipped, the sentences short as if he were conserving words and punctuated with little clicks from a set of loose-fitting dentures. "Years now."

"You look like a man who notices people. Am I right?"

"Yep. Good place to people-watch."

"Does that include deliverymen?"

"Don't discriminate. Why?"

"I'm trying to locate a man who made deliveries here a couple of years ago. May or may not still make them. Young, very fat, long hair in a ponytail. Wore a white uniform of some kind."

"Ah," the old man said.

"The description strike a chord?"

"Couldn't miss him. Big as a house."

"What did he deliver?"

"Buns. Cookies."

"For what company?"

"Sun something. Get it in a minute."

"Does he still make deliveries here?"

"Nope."

"How long since you saw him last?"

"Year, maybe two."

"You ever talk to him?"

"Don't talk, just watch."

"Hear somebody use his name?"

"Nope."

"Or notice if there was one over his uniform pocket?"

"Nope." The dentures made a sharp clicking sound. "Got it."

"Sir?"

"Company name," the old man said. "SunGold. SunGold Bakery."

SunGold Bakery Products was located in the southeastern section of the city, a block off Bayshore Boulevard. Two good-sized warehouse-type buildings connected by a short wing that fronted on the street, with a cyclone-fenced yard along one side. The wing housed the company offices, and the main entrance was there; Runyon parked in front of it, but he didn't go inside. Outfits this size had rules about employees giving out personal information, and office workers generally observed them. Deliverymen, if properly approached, weren't so apt to be close followers of company policy.

The yard gates were open and he walked in through them. A dozen or more large white vans were parked there, the SunGold emblem — a smiling face inside a sunburst — and the company name painted on their side panels. Three men were in sight, two dressed in white uniforms, one in mechanic's overalls. Runyon picked the oldest of the deliverymen, who was whistling tunelessly to himself while he checked some sort of list attached to a clipboard. Good choice. Friendly when he was approached, still friendly after the questions started. And not reticent about dispensing information.

"Sure, I know who you mean," he said. His name was Harry; it was stitched in gold thread over his uniform pocket. "How come you're looking for him?"

"I've been told that he knows someone I'm trying to find. A young woman who's gone missing."

"Is that right? I wouldn't want to get him in any trouble."

"Nothing like that. The woman's disappearance was voluntary."

"Couldn't be somebody he was dating."

"No, just a casual acquaintance."

"Uh-huh. I hate to say it, Sean's a pretty

good guy, but it's kind of hard to imagine him ever being with a woman. You know, his size. He was real self-conscious about it."

"Was?"

"Still is, I guess. He doesn't work for SunGold anymore."

"Since when?"

"Oh, must be a couple of years now."

"Quit? Fired?"

"Quit," Harry said. "Offer of a better job somewhere else."

"Do you know where?"

"No, sure don't."

"Or what kind of job?"

"Sorry. He didn't talk much, about himself or anything else."

"Shy."

"Real shy. Kind of a loner."

"The brooding type?"

"I wouldn't say that. No, he seemed pretty upbeat most of the time, usually had a smile on his face. Good guy, like I said."

"What's his last name?"

"Osgood? No, that's wrong. Something started with an O . . . Ostrow? That's it, Ostrow."

"O-s-t-r-o-w?"

"Sounds right."

"And Sean, spelled S-e-a-n or S-h-a-w-n?"

"S-e-a-n."

"Do you know where he lived?"

"Someplace over by Golden Gate Park," Harry said. "I know that because the park was on his route and sometimes he'd time his deliveries over there so he could go home for lunch. Big eater. Man, he could really pack it in."

"Any chance you could find out the address for me?"

"How would I do that? You mean check the company files?"

"I'd be willing to pay for the information."

"Hey, no, I couldn't do that," Harry said. "Not for any amount. Bosses found out, they'd throw my ass right out of here. I shouldn't even be talking to you right now."

Now he had a name. Sean Ostrow. With that and the other information Runyon had gathered, it should be relatively easy to track the man down.

Should be, but wasn't.

Back at the office, he checked the city phone directory. No listing for Sean Ostrow. The agency kept phone books for all the Bay Area cities dating back five years, and he checked each of the San Francisco books for that period. Same results. An Internet background search was the next step. He could have started one himself, but Tamara was far more skilled at that kind of thing than he was. He went to her with the need and the favor.

She said, "We're off the Troxell case. And we don't have a client to justify mixing in a homicide investigation."

"Unofficial client. My time, my expense. I told Erin Dumont's sister I'd try to help."

"Why?"

Because she looked like Colleen. Because she seemed to be stuck in his head and he couldn't get her out. He said, "Because she's the type who'll keep on grieving until there's some kind of closure. And the SFPD hasn't come up with anything in six weeks. You know what that means."

"Unsolved file."

"If it isn't there already."

Tamara sighed. "What makes you think Ostrow did that girl?"

"I don't. I think he's a possible."

"Why?"

"Everything points to an obsession killing. Love, rejection, hate, lust, remorse — all part of the pattern. And Ostrow fits the profile."

"Maybe so. But hanging around her for a month two years ago doesn't make him obsessed."

"Neither does being obese, shy, a loner.

But add them all together and you've got a possible."

"Yeah. But what doesn't add is that two-year gap. If he was so obsessed with her, how come he stayed away from her all that time? What took him so long to work up to that night in the park?"

"Could be he didn't have a choice," Runyon said.

"What, you mean he might've been locked up somewhere those two years, for some other crime?"

"Worth checking on."

But Ostrow, according to Tamara's contact at the SFPD, had no criminal record of any kind in California. A record in another state was still a possibility, but getting that information would take time.

She ran other checks. Sean David Ostrow was a member of the Teamsters Union, but obtaining personal information from a major union on one of its members was almost as impossible as obtaining it from the IRS. Under a fairly recent state law, private individuals — and that included private detective agencies — no longer had open access to DMV records. But the DMV, unlike unions, could be circumspectly breached with the right kind of know-how. Ostrow had a California driver's license, issued four years ago in San Francisco and valid for another two years. His registered vehicle was a 1988 Ford Taurus, license number 2UGK697. The first numeral and first letter matched the ones on Troxell's memory notes, but that didn't have to mean anything; 2U was a common enough prefix. His birthdate was May 14, 1979. His address was listed as 2599 Kirkham, and there had been no notification of change since the date of issue.

Runyon drove out to Kirkham Street. Number 2599 was a twelve-unit apartment building not far from Golden Gate Park, but on the opposite side several miles from where Erin Dumont and Risa Nyland lived. Ostrow's name wasn't on any of the mailboxes in the foyer. None of the other boxes bore a building manager's label, so he rang bells until he'd gone through all twelve. Three responses. A woman on the second floor said she remembered seeing Sean Ostrow in the building ("How could you miss him?"), but she hardly knew him and had no idea where he'd moved to or when. A sharp-tongued woman on the same floor said she didn't know anybody named Ostrow; she'd only lived there a year and a half, and added mistakenly that she didn't want anything to do with any goddamn salesmen. An elderly black man on the same floor said he'd known Ostrow slightly, that he was friendly enough but didn't have much to say to anybody; he'd lived there about a year and moved out abruptly "two years ago last May. I remember because it was the same week I fell and broke my hip. Asked him how come he was leaving. Said there was something he had to do and he couldn't do it in the city. Said he was going east."

"No specific place?"

"Just east, that's all."

"What was it he had to do?"

"Asked him, but he just smiled and walked away."

When Runyon got back to the agency, Tamara had more background information on Ostrow waiting for him. Most of it was routine. Born and raised in Astoria, Oregon, worked there as a beer-truck driver for a year after high school graduation. Mother deceased, father's whereabouts unknown. No criminal record in Oregon. Spotless driving record in both Oregon and California.

But there was one potential lead. Ostrow had an older sister, Arlene, married the same year he'd quit his job in Astoria. Her name was Burke now, and she and her husband had also relocated to northern California — to Santa Rosa, where they were still living.

18

The weekend started off on a troubling note and kept getting progressively worse.

Kerry was still in a funk Saturday morning. Not the withdrawn, openly depressed, gloom-dripping variety; the kind that in some ways was even worse because it was all pretense and sham. False cheerfulness. Pallid little smiles. Chatter about anything and everything except what was going on inside her head, and evasions and circumlocutions whenever I asked her a direct question or tried to draw her out. At breakfast I suggested that the three of us go for a drive down the coast, have lunch in Half Moon Bay or a picnic on one of the beaches around San Gregorio. Wonderful idea, she said, but she needed to work on one of her accounts, the Harmony Dairy account; it probably meant a trip downtown to Bates and Carpenter at some point, hadn't she mentioned this last night? Maybe tomorrow we'd go for the drive, if she could come up with the right copy for Harmony's new ad campaign by then. Or maybe Emily and I should go today, just the two of us, she didn't want to spoil our weekend just because she had to work.

She gulped coffee and excused herself and went away to her study. Her plate was still full of eggs and toast; she'd eaten no more than two bites of either. Emily looked at the plate, then looked at me with an expression of deep concern.

"Something's wrong with Mom," she said.

"I know," I said.

"What? What's the matter?"

"She won't talk to me about it."

"Me, either. I asked her, but she just changed the subject. What're we going to do?"

"Wait until she's ready to tell us. We can't force her."

"No, but . . . I'm really worried."

"So am I."

"What if it's something *serious?* What if—"

"We're not going to play the 'what if' game," I said. "All that does is make the waiting and the worrying worse."

"So we just pretend everything's okay?"

"For now, for today. How about that drive?"

"I don't feel much like it, Dad."

"It's clear here, it'll be nice down the coast."

"Can't we just stay home?"

"You can if you want to. I need to get out for a while."

Emily chewed her lip. "I guess I do, too. I guess I don't want to stay home after all."

Charles Kayabalian called at two thirty, just after Emily and I got back from lunch and a batch of errands. "Well, I wouldn't want to go through that again," he said. "Makes trial law seem like a walk in the park."

"Troxell didn't take it well?"

"Hard to say just how he took it. He didn't put out any arguments or denials, didn't seem upset by the fact that Lynn was having him followed or the contents of your report. Didn't say more than a dozen words the whole time, most of them monosyllables. He just sat there like a stunned deer. The look on his face . . . Christ."

"He agree to go to the police voluntarily?"

"Monday morning. With me along as counsel."

"Why not today or tomorrow?"

"I suggested that, get it over with as soon

as possible, but he wouldn't go for it. Needs a little time to work himself up to it, I think. The three of us tried to be gentle, but we still hit him pretty hard."

"Only three of you?"

"Lynn, Drew Casement, and myself."

"What happened to the family doctor?"

"She decided against calling him. I can't blame her."

"But Troxell did agree to get help?"

"Well, he didn't balk at the suggestion. That look on his face, the few things he said . . . poor bastard, he knows he's in a bad way."

"The sooner the better," I said. "And there should probably be eyes on him until he does."

"Lynn made him promise to stay home until Monday morning."

"But will he keep the promise."

"She and Casement will make sure he does," Kayabalian said. "She hid his car keys where he won't find them, as a precaution. The three of us talked about it afterward."

"Shaky situation, just the same."

"I know it. But what can you do in a case like this? There's only one legal issue and we've got that covered. The rest of it . . . no right way or wrong way to handle it, it's all

213

psychological and emotional gray areas. All you can do is take it slow, feel your way along, hope for the best."

Kerry had been gone when Emily and I returned; it was after five when she reappeared, laden with Chinese takeout that she'd picked up on the way home from Bates and Carpenter. Still cheerful, her smiles more genuine tonight, and full of apologies. "I know I've been in a terrible mood lately," she said at the dinner table, "and I'm sorry for taking it out on both of you. I won't keep doing that, I promise."

Fine, but then Emily asked her why she'd been in such a terrible mood. And she said, "Let's not talk about it tonight. Soon, okay? A day or two, and everything will be back to normal."

"You promise that, too?"

"Yes, honey. I do."

Big smile to go with the words, but it was a pretender's smile that said the promise was built less on certainty than on hope.

The phone rang at seven thirty that evening. I was closest to it when it went off, so I picked up. And the caller was the last person I expected to hear from, this night or any other.

"This is James Troxell."

After a couple of seconds I said slowly, to keep the surprise out of my voice, "Yes, Mr. Troxell. What can I do for you?"

"I've been reading your report to my wife," he said. Deep voice, calm, measured, lacking any discernible emotion. "It's very thorough, very detailed. Very revealing, too."

"Yes?"

"I feel that I ought to thank you."

"For what?"

"For helping me open my eyes. You must have found my actions bizarre. I find them bizarre myself, seeing them outlined in cold type."

What can you say to that?

"It's as though I've been wandering in a daze the past few weeks," Troxell said. "But I'm seeing and thinking clearly now."

"I'm glad to hear it. But I'm not the person you should be thanking."

"You could have gone directly to the police. You didn't have to allow me a grace period to do what I should have done in the beginning. I'm grateful that you did."

I said, "Charles Kayabalian tells me you'll be going in on Monday morning."

"That's the plan, yes."

"It won't be as difficult as you might expect."

"No, I don't think it will be. Once you finally understand and accept what has to be done, you wonder why you fought against it for so long. With help you can find the courage to go through with it."

"Yes."

"And I have all the help I need now. No more bizarre behavior, I promise you that."

"I don't understand. Why promise me?"

"It won't be necessary for you to keep watch on me any longer."

"You think you're still under surveillance? Not by us."

"You're still working for Lynn, aren't you?"

"No. Didn't she tell you?"

"Nothing was said. I just assumed you were."

"Not since yesterday morning. That report is final."

"I see," Troxell said. "Were you paid for your services?"

"In full."

"Well, then. There doesn't seem to be anything else to say, does there. Except thank you again."

"Good luck, Mr. Troxell. I hope everything works out for you."

"It will," he said.

Strange, awkward conversation. The

216

more I replayed it in my head, the odder it seemed. Something not quite right about it, off-kilter, disconnected, like a conversation in a dream. I was already on edge because of the situation with Kerry, and Troxell's call sharpened it. I felt that I ought to do something. Call Lynn Troxell, call Kayabalian . . .

But what could I say to them that would help the situation, make a difference? Or do anything except stir up the pot again?

19

Jake Runyon

The days of his life, now that Colleen was gone, were all the same — in essence if not in detail. He arranged them so that they marched by in structured uniformity, with a kind of military precision. There were no holidays, vacation days, leisurely weekends. There were only work days and make-work days and preparing-for-work days. It wasn't that he lived to work; it was that he worked because it was the only way he could live.

This Saturday was a specific-job day. Even if it hadn't been, even if Santa Rosa were hundreds of miles north of the city instead of only fifty-some, he would've been on the move by eight a.m. Part of the regimen was that he never slept in, never stayed in the apartment past eight on any morning. Movement was preferable to stasis or confinement, always.

The man who opened the door at Sean Ostrow's sister's west-side apartment was drunk. Ten o'clock on a Saturday morning, and already he had to hang on to the door and lean a shoulder against the jamb to hold himself steady. Beer-drinker, the saturation type: he had a sixteen-ounce can of cheap malt liquor in one hand and the smell of it came from his pores as well as his open mouth. Early thirties, heavyset, the kind of beer gut that wobbled and shimmied when he moved; unshaven, wearing a stained undershirt and a pair of faded dungarees with the fly partially unzipped. Derelict in training.

He squinted at Runyon through eyes like sliced marbles crosshatched with red lines. "Who're you?"

"Is Arlene Burke home?"

"Fuckin' salesman." The door started to close, but Runyon got a foot in the way. "Hey, what's the idea?"

"I'm not a salesman," Runyon said. "Are you Eugene Burke?"

"Who wants to know?"

"My name is Runyon. I'm trying to find Sean Ostrow —"

"Huh?"

"Mrs. Burke's brother, Sean Ostrow."

"That freeloader." Burke made a sneering mouth, belched in Runyon's face, and sneered again. "Gone now and he better not come back."

"When did he leave?"

"Who the hell counts days?"

"How long was he here?"

"Too long, man."

"How long is too long?"

"Wasn't my idea to let him move in," Burke said. Then, in a blurry falsetto, " 'Get a job, bring in some money, then you can run things round here.' That's what she said to me, always throwing it in my face like it's *my* fault I can't find work. Fuckin' cow."

"Where's Ostrow now? Where did he move to?"

"So he paid a few bucks toward the rent, so what? Still a goddamn freeloader. Apartment's too small for *two* people, for Chrissake."

"Where can I find him?"

"How the hell should I know?"

"Does your wife know?"

"She don't know jack shit, that's what she don't know."

"Is she here?"

"No, she's not here, she's workin' today." Self-pity changed the timbre of his voice, put a whine in it. "Used to be Saturdays, weekends, were the best time, plenty to do, places to go, but not no more. Nothing to do but watch the tube, suck down some brews.

Too many businesses closed so you can't even go out and look for a job."

"Where does she work?"

"Huh?"

"Your wife. Where does she work?"

Burke squinted at him again. "Who the hell're you, anyway? Comin' around here, askin' about my wife?"

"Where does she work?"

"None of your business." He tried to close the door again. "Hey, move your goddamn foot."

"Not until you answer my question."

"Want me to move it for you?"

"You don't want to try that, Mr. Burke."

"No, huh?"

"No. Where does your wife work?"

Truculent glare. But when Burke finished measuring him with his blood-flecked eyes, a process that took less than ten seconds, the truculence morphed into sullen resentment. He made a disgusted sound and helped himself to a long swig from the can of malt liquor. He said then, growling the words, "Macy's. Downtown."

"Which department?"

"Housewares. You satisfied now?"

Runyon withdrew his foot.

Predictably Burke said, "Fuck you, man!" and slammed the door, fast.

★ ★ ★

Santa Rosa was a small country town, the Sonoma County seat, that had grown up too fast into a sprawling city with a population of a quarter of a million. Its "historic" downtown had been designed around a courthouse square; the county offices had been relocated elsewhere long ago and what had probably once been a quiet town center was now traffic-clogged, noisy, and spotted with indicators of encroaching urban blight. Between the square and the freeway that bisected the city, an enclosed shopping mall sprawled over two or three blocks. An attendant in the service station where Runyon stopped for gas told him that was where Macy's was located.

The usual Saturday crowds roamed the store, but most of the shoppers seemed to be in the clothing departments. There were only two browsers in housewares on the third floor, and nobody at the sales counter except a woman clerk who turned out to be Arlene Burke. Large sandy-haired woman, overweight but with a big-boned frame that carried the extra pounds gracefully enough. Tired eyes, tired face, but the weariness wasn't the kind caused by overwork or lack of sleep; it had its roots in dead dreams and shattered expectations and an out-of-work, out-of-love drunk who thought of her as a cow.

Runyon's preliminary questions put her on edge. "Sean's not in any trouble, is he?"

"Do you think he might be?"

"No, no. It's just I haven't heard from him in a while. . . . Why are you looking for my brother?"

He gave her the same story he'd used on the SunGold driver. "How long since you had contact with him?"

"More than two months now."

"From the time he moved out of your apartment?"

"That's right."

"Do you know where he went?"

"Back to San Francisco. He got a new apartment and a new job there."

"Where in San Francisco?"

"He didn't tell me. Sometimes Sean can be . . . well, private."

"Did he say what kind of job?"

"No. He said he'd give me all the details later, but he . . . not a word since he left."

"Can you think of any reason for that?"

"No, unless things didn't work out down there and he decided to move away again. He's always had terrible luck with jobs and his personal life . . . it turned him into a wanderer. This time, though . . . he's changed so much, all for the better, and he really does seem ready to settle down."

"In San Francisco?"

"I hope so. I had the idea he'd met someone there."

"A woman, you mean?"

"Yes."

"Did you ask him if he had?"

"I did," she said, "but he just smiled and said he wasn't ready to talk about it yet." Pause. "It couldn't be the woman you're looking for, could it?"

Runyon said, "Maybe. Does the name Erin Dumont mean anything to you?"

"Erin Dumont . . . no. Is that her name?"

"You're sure he never mentioned her?"

"Positive. Sean's never talked about any woman with me."

"When did you get the idea he'd met someone?"

"Not long before he moved out. He was so happy — a new man, so totally different from the Sean I grew up with. A lot more . . . confident is the word, I guess. I could see it as soon as he came here from Sacramento."

"When was that?"

"A year ago this past February."

"How long was he in Sacramento?"

"Not long. Nine or ten months."

"So he moved up there right after he quit his job with SunGold Bakery."

"That's right."

"Do you know why he quit SunGold, left San Francisco?"

"Not really. A wanderer, like I said."

"Where did he work in Sacramento?"

"I don't know. Some sort of driving job."

"Did he live with you the entire time he was in Santa Rosa?"

"Lord, no," she said. "My husband would never have stood for that, he made enough of a fuss having Sean around for a month. No, Sean had his own apartment over by the fairgrounds until the lease ran out. He tried to arrange to stay on for one more month, until he could move into his new place in the city, but the landlord wouldn't agree to it. So I talked Gene, that's my husband, into letting him stay with us."

"What was his job here?"

"Avondale Electric. They manufacture solenoid valves — he worked in their warehouse and made deliveries."

"Avondale is located where?"

"On Petaluma Hill Road, do you know where that is?"

"Yes. Did Sean have any friends in Santa Rosa, somebody from work he hung around with?"

"Not that I know about. He doesn't make friends easily — he's always been shy, doesn't relate well to other people. Women especially."

"So he didn't date much."

"Not at all when we were kids. He seemed almost afraid of girls after that time he was expelled from high school. If he did finally meet someone, I couldn't be happier for him."

"Why was he expelled?"

"For fighting. It wasn't his fault, he'd worked up enough nerve to talk to a girl he liked and the little bitch laughed at him and some of the boys overheard and started taunting him. Sean is easygoing but when he's pushed too far . . . well, he has a temper."

"Violent temper?"

"Just a temper. I have one, too, when I'm picked on." Her mouth made a lemony pucker. "The Ostracized Ostrows."

"Pardon?"

"The Ostracized Ostrows. That's what we called ourselves. Neither of us was popular growing up, Sean because he was so heavy and me because . . ." She broke off, nibbled flecks of dark red off her lower lip — embarrassed now. "I shouldn't be talking like this, to a stranger. And I really should get out on the floor and do some rearranging and re-stocking. If the supervisor comes by and catches me wasting time . . ."

"Just a couple more questions. Does your brother still drive a brown, eighty-eight Ford Taurus, license number 2UGK697?"

"Still does. It's old but he keeps it in good condition."

"Do you have a photograph of him I could borrow?"

"A photograph? Well, not with me. And not a recent one."

"Even an old one might help."

"Well . . . I could look when I get home. But that won't be until late — I'm on over-time tonight."

"I'd appreciate it. My cell phone num-ber's on the card I gave you. If you have a photo, I could come by tomorrow and pick it up."

"All the way from San Francisco again? On Sunday?"

"I'm on overtime myself this weekend."

"All right," she said. "If you'll do me a favor when you find Sean."

"If I can."

"Ask him to call me? And let me know yourself if everything's all right with him? I really am starting to worry." She sighed heavily, and the lines of weary resignation in her face seemed deeper as she said, "Poor Sean, nothing ever seems to work out for him. I had so much hope this time . . . so much hope for one of us . . ."

Avondale Electric was open on Saturday. Runyon talked to a woman in the office and a man in the warehouse; both had good things to say about Sean Ostrow's job performance, but nothing at all to tell him about Ostrow's present whereabouts or the new job in the city. If he'd used Avondale as a reference, his new employer hadn't seen fit to follow up.

The residential section where Ostrow had lived in Santa Rosa, between the county fairgrounds and Luther Burbank Park, was close by. Runyon drove over there, even though he knew it would be wasted effort. And it was. He spent an hour at the apartment building and in the neighborhood looking for somebody who'd known Ostrow, and couldn't even find one person who remembered him.

Half the day still lay ahead of him. He drove around Santa Rosa for a time, then took Highway 101 to the small towns that lay to the north. Windsor was a newish collection of tract houses and shopping malls,

Healdsburg an old tourist-laden wine-country town built around a square, Geyserville a wine-country village without the tourists or the square. He didn't stay long in any of them, just enough time to mark and memorize the territory. From Geyserville he went west through a long valley filled with vineyards, small wineries, and droves of early summer tourists, then up around Lake Sonoma, then south through a different part of Dry Creek Valley and back to Santa Rosa.

Still only four o'clock. He could hang around up here and if Ostrow's sister called and had a photograph, he could go pick it up. No. He'd had enough of the North Bay and its backroads for one day, and there was still Sunday to get through. He drove back down 101 to the city.

When he came through the toll plaza on the bridge, he took Lincoln Boulevard down through the Presidio. Even before he reached Sea Cliff and Twenty-fifth Avenue, he knew where he was going without thinking about it.

Risa Niland lived a block off Geary and another block from Washington High School. He turned up Thirtieth Avenue past the school's athletic fields. In big letters strung across the front of the stadium entrance on that side were the words OF ALL VICTORIES THE FIRST AND GREATEST IS FOR MAN TO CONQUER HIMSELF — PLATO. Nice sentiment, but how many students paid attention to it, took it to heart? Safe bet that it wasn't many. For that matter how many people could look back on their lives from any age and say honestly that they'd conquered themselves? Not him, for damn sure.

The three-story building at the corner of Anza and Twenty-ninth was peach-colored stucco with a tile roof and an old-fashioned canopy over the entrance. Two apartments per floor, from the size of it. He saw all of that as he approached the corner; he didn't see her until he braked at the stop sign.

Even at a distance he recognized her — the resemblance to Colleen was like a beacon. She was standing just outside the canopy, dressed in jeans and a red pullover, her red-gold hair bound up in a roll, talking to a young, fair-haired, linebacker type in jogging sweats. The guy said something to her that made her reach out and touch his arm. Friends, maybe more than friends. Maybe even the ex-husband.

Runyon might have stopped if she'd been alone. As it was, he made the turn and drove on by. Neither Risa nor the man glanced his way, and he didn't look back at them in the rearview mirror. None of his business. Her personal life had nothing to do with him.

Automatic pilot again. Through the park, east on Lincoln to Stanyan, down Seventeenth to the Castro district and up to Hartford Street just off Twentieth, past the Stick Victorian where Joshua lived with his faithless boyfriend, Kenneth. Nobody on the sidewalk here, no sign of his son, and what if there had been? Four months since he'd seen or had any contact with him. Joshua had had plenty to say in March, when the pair of gay-bashers beat up Kenneth and put him in the hospital; he'd needed his father then, to help find the men responsible, and he'd permitted an uneasy truce. But once the need had been filled and the gay-bashers put out of commission — silence. The old hatreds instilled by his mother had rebuilt the wall between them thicker and higher than ever.

So what was the sense coming here? Or in the drive-by at Risa Niland's building? No sense. He got out of the Castro, backtracked over Twin Peaks and down to Nineteenth Avenue. Ate a tasteless dinner at a coffee shop — he had no appetite for Chinese food tonight. And went from there to his apartment, because it was nearly eight and he was tired and because he had nowhere else to go. And as soon as he walked into that cold, impersonal space a sudden wave of feeling came from somewhere inside him, so intense it made him catch his breath. It didn't last long; he didn't let it last long. But the memory of it lingered like a bitter taste in his mouth.

Alone.

And lonely.

20
Tamara

Saturday night she almost got laid.

Almost: The Sad, Pathetic Story of Tamara Corbin's Love Life.

Almost messed up and almost pregnant by one of a succession of losers in high school. Almost permanent relationship with the almost love of her life. Almost sex with a man she almost hadn't gone out with in the first place. And the reason for Saturday night's almost —

Lord!

Man wasn't a pickup, he was an actual date. First date she'd had with anybody except Horace since her first semester at S.F. State. Blind date, which was the reason she almost hadn't gone out with him. Vonda was responsible. She got together with the girlfriend for a drink after work on Friday, poured out her tale of Horace woe, and the first thing Vonda said was, "Only way to forget a man is to find yourself another one quick." Then she'd gone and done something about it, quick; Vonda never wasted any time when it came to men. By nine o'clock Friday night, the blind date was all arranged.

His name was Clement Rawls, he was a stockbroker with the same company Vonda's boyfriend, Ben Sherman, worked for. Ben was white — and Jewish, leave it to Vonda — and if Clement had been either or both of the same she would probably have said no. Not that she had anything in principle against dating white guys or Jewish guys, but she'd never done it and this wasn't the time to start. But no, Clement was African-American. A hunk, Vonda said, and to her surprise he'd turned out to be just that. Few years older than her, nice smile, sexy eyes, the Denzel type. Cool, easy to talk to, funny, didn't come on too strong. Only thing wrong with him — the only thing, anyway, until the kink he revealed to her when they were alone together — was that he was hung up on his appearance and pretty fond of himself. Metrosexuals didn't appeal to her; Mr. Clement Rawls would've eventually tied her patience in a knot. But he was no more interested in a long-term relationship than she was, and for one night it didn't really matter.

He picked her up at her apartment — he drove a Beamer, what else? — and they went out to dinner and then club-crawling in SoMa with Vonda and Ben. About an hour with him was all it took to break down her resolve against any more casual sex. Love and respect and all that were fine, but when your hormones were running wild everything else took second place to scratching the itch. He was a terrific dancer and a terrific kisser, a combination that told her he'd be good in bed and got her even more hotted up. When he finally took her home she hadn't had any last-minute hesitations about inviting him in.

Should've figured he was too good to be true. Should've had a clue when he dragged his briefcase out of the backseat and brought it in with him, but she figured as self-confident as he was, he expected to spend the night and the briefcase contained his toothbrush and a change of underwear. Wrong. Wrong big time.

Everything went along fine for a while. They drank some more wine and made out on the couch, both of them getting their temperatures raised — man really did know how to kiss. So then she said, "Come on in the bedroom, Clement," and they got up and swapped some more spit and she started leading him into the other room.

And then it all fell apart. He unlocked

their lips and whispered in her ear, "Before we go to bed, there's something I'd like you to do. Something, well, special to please me."

Uh-oh. "What kind of special?"

"It's nothing, really. You won't mind."

"If you want to tie me up —"

"No."

"Or lick Cool Whip off my —"

"No, no."

"I'm not into games. Or pain, I draw the line at pain."

"Nothing like that, I promise."

"What, then?"

"I'll show you."

He let go of her, put his hands on that briefcase of his instead, and showed her. Whipped this thing out of there that for a couple of awful seconds looked like some kind of dead animal.

"Yo, what *is* that?"

He shook it out, extended it toward her. Long and blond and hairy —

"A wig?" she said.

"A wig," he said.

That was what it was, all right. About three feet of blond hair so pale it was almost platinum, straight except for some tangles and end flips. She stared at it hanging from his fingers like some kind of trophy scalp.

He was staring at it, too, hot-eyed, his mouth hanging open a little as if he might start drooling on it.

"What you want me to do with that?"

"Wear it," he said.

"You don't mean in bed while we — ?"

"Yes."

"Man, what for?"

"It excites me."

". . . Yeah, so I see."

He wiggled the wig. "Put it on," he said.

"No," she said.

"You won't be sorry. It enhances my performance."

"Not gonna be any performance with that thing on my head."

"Come on, now, it's just a harmless fantasy —"

"I don't do fantasies. I don't do wigs."

"The sex will be fantastic, you'll see. Best you've ever had."

"Oh, sure. Blondes have more fun, right?"

"Don't you want to find out?"

"Uh-uh. No way."

"Tamara, it's important to me that you wear it."

"Must be. What, you carry it with you everywhere you go, just in case you get lucky?"

"I won't dignify that question with an answer."

"Dignify? I don't see much dignity in a black man hauling a Marilyn Monroe scalp around in his briefcase."

"It's just a wig. You make it sound like something obscene."

"It is if you don't wash it."

"What?"

"Bet you never wash it. Expect me to put it on *my* head with all your other women's cooties still in there."

"For God's sake —"

"Listen here. You want a white woman, why don't you go find yourself one instead of messing with me?"

"I don't want a white woman. I don't date white women."

"Black woman in a blond wig? That what boils your pot?"

He blinked. His mouth thinned down tight. The wig wiggled. "There's nothing wrong with that."

"Any black woman, right? Just so long as she's wearing Marilyn's hair."

"This isn't Marilyn's hair!"

"Looks like it from where I'm standing."

"And you're wrong, it's you I want —"

"You sure about that?"

"What do you mean, am I sure?"

"Can't help but wonder."

"Wonder what?"

"If it's a woman you *really* want. Or just that scalp."

He puffed up like a toad and made a couple of sputtering sounds.

She was on a roll now. No longer horny, no longer interested in Mr. Clement Rawls, and with her claws out in frustration. She said, "You ask me, you're in love with that thing. The way you hold it, look at it, practically drool on it. Wouldn't surprise me if you pet it and hump it all by itself when there's nobody else around."

"You can't talk to me like that! You smart-ass bitch, who do you think you are!"

That was when she threw him out.

And that was the end of that.

Sad and pathetic, all right. But the worst thing about this Saturday night almost, aside from the fact she hadn't gotten laid, was that now her story had a new twist that made her feel sorry for herself in a different way. A cheating chump cellist wasn't bad enough, oh no. Now the Man Upstairs had to go and throw in a scalp-sucking stock-broker fool and turn a tragedy into a Whoopi Goldberg farce.

21

I was driving down a dark, twisty road, going somewhere in a hurry. Trees, houses, fence posts materialized and dematerialized like wraiths in the stabbing headlight glare. There were other people crowded into the car with me, front seat and back; I couldn't see their faces in the blackness, but I could feel them close around me, somebody's fetid breath moist on the back of my neck. I was sweating from all the body heat. A dis-embodied voice kept saying, "Slow down, slow down, slow down," and I kept driving fast, rustlings and whisperings all around me as the clutch of passengers shifted posi-tion.

Up ahead something took on sudden defi-nition in the headlights: railroad tracks, flashing red semaphore lights, a crossing arm that was just starting to come down across the road. One of the faceless people shouted, "Look out! Train coming!" An-other one in the backseat threw an arm around my neck and yanked my head back. I struggled to loosen the grip so I could breathe. And then I could see the eye of the locomotive bearing down from the left, big and bright like a madman's eye, growing larger and larger until it took away most of the dark. I hit the brakes, hard. The car slewed, skidded, came back on a point. Warning bells began to clang as I brought us to a grinding stop nose up to the crossing arm. The locomotive was a roaring giant now, its headlamp as painfully blinding as the sun at midday, and the bells kept clanging and jangling —

One of the faceless women said, "Who's that at this hour?"

I said, "What? What?"

Kerry said, "The phone, there's somebody on the phone."

And I was sitting up in bed, damp and disoriented, part of the sheet in a stranglehold around my neck. The lamp on Kerry's nightstand was on; the light made me squint. I fought off the sheet and blanket, fought off the remnants of the dream, and got my hand on the phone and finally shut off the noise.

I growled something half coherent into the receiver. A woman's voice said my name, then rushed into an apology for calling so late, and then there was a jumble of words that didn't signify. What did come through was the emotion behind them: they were soaked in the raw fluids of panic.

"Slow down," I said, "I can't understand you. Who is this?"

"Lynn Troxell." Raggedy breath. "Oh God, I didn't know who else to call. . . ."

That got rid of most of the sleep fuzz. "What is it, what's happened?"

"It's Jim, he's gone."

"What do you mean, gone?"

"A few minutes ago. I woke up, he wasn't in bed, and then I heard his car. I don't know how he could have found the keys but he must have, I hid his spare set, too. . . ."

The red numerals on the nightstand clock swam into focus: 12:57. Sunday night, Monday morning.

"He's going to kill himself," she said.

Christ! Completely awake now, the night sweat cold on my back and under my arms. "What makes you think that?"

"He left me a note."

"Saying what, exactly?"

" 'I'm so sorry for all the pain. Please forgive me.' "

"Nothing else?"

"Just 'all my love' and his signature. He never writes notes, it can't be anything but . . ." Another raggedy breath. "I thought he was all right, he seemed all right. Drew talked to him for a long time this afternoon and said he seemed all right . . . oh God, I don't know what to do . . ."

"Have you notified the police?"

"I wanted to, but . . . no, I called Drew first and he said the note isn't enough for them to do anything, it's too vague, it doesn't mention suicide. . . ."

He was right about that. A 911 call wouldn't have bought her anything but frustration and more panic.

"He thought maybe the place on Potrero Hill, he's on his way there now, but what if Jim isn't there? I can't think where else he might have gone. . . ."

I could; I had a better idea than Casement's. I said, "I'll see what I can do to find him, Mrs. Troxell."

"Will you? I know it's not your problem anymore, but I didn't know who else to call. . . . You'll let me know right away, no matter what?"

"Right away. You have my cell phone number if you hear anything first. Meanwhile, try to stay calm."

"Calm," she said. "Yes, all right, yes."

Kerry had picked up enough from my end of the conversation to understand what was going on. She said as I yanked on my pants, "Is there anything I can do?"

"No. One of us chasing around in the night is enough."

"Is there anything you can do?"

"If there is," I said, "it shouldn't take long to find out."

Ocean Beach.

That seemed the most likely place he'd head for. Not Potrero Hill. Troxell was a neat, almost fastidious individual, conscious of the feelings of others; he wouldn't want to clutter up the Lindens' lives by doing the dutch in their backyard. His wife had said yesterday that he was drawn to water, and the beach, the Pacific were a magnetic pull; he'd already been out there twice this week. Walk into the ocean, maybe, let the undertow drag him out; hypothermia would make the drowning fairly quick. Neat, clean. From his point of view, anyway.

Suicide. Building to it, planning it all along. That was the reason for his call Saturday evening. In his careful way he'd wanted to make sure he wasn't still being watched, followed. The thank-yous and explanations had been sincere enough but nothing more than camouflage. Hell, I'd known it at the time. Refused to admit it to myself because I couldn't be sure and there hadn't been anything I could do about it. You can't stop a person from plotting to do away with himself, any more than you can stop a person from plotting a crime, until it reaches the commission stage. Something I could do now, if it wasn't too late, but even then it might only be a stopgap measure. If a suicide case is determined enough, nobody — not a loved one and especially not a stranger — can prevent him from going through with it sooner or later. Still, you have to try. As long as he's alive there's hope he can be saved. Even if there wasn't you'd still have to try.

As soon as I was in the car and rolling I used my cell phone to call Jake Runyon. I didn't like dragging him out of bed, but it was necessary and I knew he wouldn't mind. A night call woke him up a lot faster than it did me; he was alert and responsive within seconds. Three sentences were enough to tell him what was going down and what I suspected.

He said, "Lloyd Lake's another possibility. That's where he saw the abduction."

"Christ, I didn't even think of that. You're right, he might be drawn back there. But I still think it's the beach."

"I'll swing through the park first and check it out."

"Okay. I'm on Portola now, heading for Sloat, so I'll cover the south end of the beach. If he's not at Lloyd Lake, you head for Cliff House and work on down the Great Highway."

Traffic was light; I drove faster, risked running one of the lights on Portola Drive. There might still be time. If Troxell didn't act immediately; if he stuttered out there on the beach, like the ones who crawl into bathtubs with a razor blade often do with their hesitation cuts. It all depended on how intent he was, how far he'd stepped over the line.

Sometimes you make the right guesses. The first place I went to was the beachfront parking area at the foot of Sloat Boulevard, because it was the closest section of Ocean Beach to both St. Francis Wood and Diamond Heights, and because it had been Troxell's Thursday night destination. His destination this time, too, by God. The only car on the sandswept asphalt out there was his silver BMW.

I almost missed it; would have if I hadn't driven through the horseshoe turnaround at the entrance and into the lot itself. It was drawn in close alongside the old building that housed public restrooms, all but the rear deck invisible in the thick shadows. I cut in next to it, dragged the six-cell flashlight from under the dash before I jumped out.

He hadn't bothered to lock the driver's door. I leaned in, flashed the light front and back. Empty.

The tide was in and the wind was up as it had been all week; the breakers rolling in off high, choppy seas made a steady roaring noise like the oncoming locomotive in my dream. The pavement was drifted with sand; I had to pick my way across to the beach side of the lot to keep from slipping. The moon was out, but high running clouds kept hiding and then revealing it — shine, dark, shine, dark, like an erratic neon sign blinking on and off. In the seconds it shone, I could see the beach for a few hundred yards in both directions. He wasn't on it. Nothing was on it, not even a seabird.

I buttoned my overcoat collar to the throat, pulled on the gloves I'd jammed into a pocket, and climbed over the wire guardrail. The earth shelved off abruptly here, in a series of short drop-offs and rock-and-sand declivities; I used the flash to pick my way down onto the beach. The wind, heavy with the smell of brine, flung stinging grit into my face and eyes as I slogged through loose, dry sand. Down here the crash of surf was thunderous. Big waves, white-foamed and angry-looking, spread fans of dirty spume over two-thirds of the beach's width.

If Troxell had walked out into that pounding surf, he'd have been dead in less than a minute. Sucked out by the undertow and carried away, what was left of him to be deposited here or somewhere else up or down the coast when the sea was calm again.

The hesitation possibility took me to the upper edge of the surf line, along it a ways to the south and then back in the opposite direction. The ebb and flow of the breakers would have erased any close marks, but back up here there was a chance of finding some indication of recent passage. But there wasn't any. No footprints anywhere in the wet sand; it was as darkly smooth and glistening as white-rimmed black glass.

Salt spray caked my face now. Particles of sand had gotten into my left eye and set up a burning so sharp I had to keep it squeezed shut. The wind cut through the layers of clothing I wore, seemed to lay a sheeting of ice over my flesh. Give it up, I thought, before you catch pneumonia. But my legs weren't listening. They kept slogging me forward, beyond the entrance to the parking lot toward the skeletal remains of an old pier farther up the beach.

The wet sand remained smooth, un-broken.

A sudden gust blew up a whirlwind of sand; I managed to get my head and body turned in time to keep most of it out of my face. In that same moment the moon appeared from behind a rampart of clouds. When I opened my good eye I had a clear look at the series of low, grass-crested dunes that stretched away close to the Great Highway. The moonglow painted their slopes white — empty white, all except one. That one, close beyond the parking area, had a blob of something dark and elongated on it about halfway up.

I squinted, moving forward to try to get a better look. Man-sized blob, a shorter elongation jutting out to one side that might have been a leg.

The moon vanished again. Darkness shrouded the dunes; all I could see over there was the backwash of lights along the Great Highway and Sloat Boulevard. The flash beam wasn't strong enough to reach that far. I tramped that way as fast as I could, the wind giving me a good push from behind. By the time I neared the foot of the dune I was panting and shivering. I switched on the six-cell again, laid its light on the back-sprawled shape.

Too late. Already too late when I arrived at the beach, by maybe fifteen minutes.

Troxell's eyes were open wide, their view of eternity obscured by a film of blown sand. Small wound on his right temple, the blood still glistening wet there and where it was spotted on the sand near his head.

I'd been wrong about him letting the sea take him out. That hadn't been his intention at all. He'd walked straight over here from the parking lot — the single line of his foot-prints was still visible — and sat down on this sheltered dune with the highway hidden behind him to avoid any possible interference. And then, for whatever skewed reasons, the man who'd been a vocal advocate of gun control had blown his brains out with a small-caliber pistol.

22

I said, "Poor miserable bastard."

Runyon said, "At least he's not hurting anymore."

"That sounds like you approve of suicide."

"Not a matter of approval. Let's say I understand the impulse."

I let that go. Maybe he'd entertained the idea himself after his wife's slow, painful death; I did not want to know. Suicide was an alien concept to me. I'd seen too much death, spent too much time trying to keep myself and others alive; life was too important to me to see it thrown away on a selfish and cowardly act. Maybe Troxell wasn't hurting anymore, but his wife damn well would be for a long time to come. As far as I was concerned he'd had no right to do that to someone he professed to love, to any survivor who had to keep on with the hard business of living.

We were standing on the dune, on either side of what was left of James Troxell, both of us with flashlights. I'd notified the 911 dispatcher before calling Runyon, but he had been up by the Beach Chalet, not far away, and he'd gotten here first. Nonemergency 911 calls take a while to bring a response, even late at night, in these emergency-glutted times.

He put his light on the small weapon in the dead man's hand. It threw cold glints off the metal frame. "Twenty-two semi-auto."

"Target pistol."

"Yeah. Looks new."

"Bought for the occasion," I said. "He didn't own a gun before. Didn't like guns, from what I was told."

"Funny way to take himself out then."

"Making some kind of statement. Or because it was the quickest way."

"Takes guts to shoot yourself in the head," Runyon said.

"Not if you want to die badly enough."

Neither of us held our lights on the dead face, but I could see it well enough in the overspill from where the beams were pointed. I shut mine off, turned my back to the corpse. The sea continued to hammer at the beach, the larger breakers throwing up jets of faintly luminescent mist as they came crashing down. The wind seemed stronger now; it had erased Troxell's footprints, was filling in most of mine and Runyon's. I was so cold I couldn't feel my nose and ears when I touched them.

Runyon asked, "So where does this leave us on the Dumont homicide?"

"Good question. I'll talk to Jack Logan first thing in the morning. He'll chew my ass for allowing the weekend grace period, but if we're lucky that'll be the end of it. We're covered as long as the Lindens don't say anything when the law comes around and finds what you found."

"They'll keep quiet. Last thing they want is trouble."

"No pressure on them to give up that key, right?"

"No. I was careful about that. There's no reason for them to turn on me."

"Unless the illegal rental angle comes out some way. Never know how people will react when their little scams blow up in their faces. Sometimes it makes them vindictive as hell."

Runyon had nothing to say to that. He knew the truth of it as well as I did.

I watched the ocean for a time, the constant shifting from oily black to light-striped gray as the moon and the running clouds played around overhead. "I wish I knew if

Troxell knew any more about the homicide than he wrote down."

"We'll never know, now."

"What's your guess?"

"He didn't."

"Mine, too. But that could just be wishful thinking."

Other sounds rose above the pound of the surf: more than one vehicle turning off the Great Highway into the horseshoe entrance to the parking lot. Swirls of red light put a bloody shine on the sky in that direction.

"Here we go," I said.

We spent another long, cold hour and a half up there with uniformed cops and then a team of plainclothes homicide inspectors, none of whom I knew but one of whom, the older of the inspectors, recognized my name. I did most of the talking. There wasn't any hassle, just the usual time-consuming, crime-scene grind of repetitive Q and A — all very routine and professionally handled. An ambulance showed up halfway through and a pair of attendants slogged off and then slogged back with the clay shell of James Troxell encased in a black body bag. That was all very routine and professional, too. No muss, no fuss. Every man who dies in the city, no matter who he is or how he ends his life, is treated the same: get the remains under wraps and on ice as quickly as possible, so the living don't have to face yet another reminder of their own mortality.

I asked the older inspector if it would be all right if I notified the widow. I wouldn't have done it if this had been a homicide, or if there had been doubt that it was anything but a suicide; the book says there has to be an official notification of next of kin in cases like that. But there's usually some latitude in a cut-and-dried suicide. No cop wants to break that kind of news if he can avoid it; it's one of the hardest and most thankless jobs in police work. I hated the prospect myself, but I felt I ought to do it because I was involved and because Lynn Troxell had called me for help and because I was the one who'd found the body. Moral responsibility, if nothing else.

The inspector tried not to look relieved. If I wanted the job, he said, I was welcome to it. Just make sure the widow showed up to ID the remains within twenty-four hours. I said I would.

We dispersed not long after that. Runyon went to his apartment, the cops went back to their mean streets, Troxell went to the morgue, and I went to St. Francis Wood. On the way I called Charles Kayabalian and notified him, too. One more lousy task that I felt obligated to handle.

Drew Casement opened the door at the Troxell home. Face black-rimmed with beard stubble, hair uncombed, athlete's body slumped a little inside faded Levis and a heavy sweater. And a grim ramble of words once I was inside: "I made Lynn take a Valium and lie down, she's frantic, exhausted. You didn't find him, right? He wasn't at the place on Potrero Hill, I don't know where the hell he could be. I thought it would be best if I came here instead of chasing around the city, I didn't want Lynn to be alone at a time like this —"

"I found him," I said.

". . . What?"

"I found him."

"Where?"

"Ocean Beach."

"Ocean Beach. Jesus, I should've thought of that myself —"

"He's dead, isn't he."

Those words came from Lynn Troxell in a flat, empty voice. She was standing in the doorway to the formal living room, barefoot but dressed under a loose-fitting terrycloth robe, her face pale and her eyes starry and unblinking. Composed, with no outward signs of the earlier turmoil. The Valium, maybe. But more likely it was hopeless resignation, the ashes of panic in this kind of situation.

"Yes," I said. "I'm sorry, Mrs. Troxell."

She sagged a little against the doorjamb. Otherwise, no reaction.

Casement went to her, put his arm around her as if to hold her up. She didn't seem to notice he was there. He said to me, "How did you find him?"

"Does that matter?"

"No, no, I just . . ." He shook his head.

Mrs. Troxell said in that same flat, empty voice, "How?"

"That doesn't matter, either, right now."

"Please. I want to know."

"He shot himself."

"He . . . shot . . . That can't be right . . ."

"There's no doubt."

"Why would he do that? He didn't own a gun. He wouldn't have a gun in the house."

"He was sick," Casement said, "he wanted to die. Get it over with quick. A pistol . . . that's as quick as it gets."

"Where would he get a gun?"

"Bought it somewhere, a gun shop . . ."

She shook her head, a meaningless, loose-necked movement.

"Lynn, maybe you should lie down again."

"No," she said. "I want to see him."

"Christ, you don't want to do that, not now —"

"I want to see him." She asked me, "He's not still at the beach? You didn't just leave him there?"

"No, of course not. I called the police as soon as I found him."

"You should have called us, too," Casement said.

I ignored that. So did Mrs. Troxell.

She said, "And they . . . took him away?"

"Yes."

"Where?"

"The city morgue."

"Where's that?"

"Basement of the Hall of Justice."

"They'll let me see him?"

"Yes. You'll need to make an official identification."

Casement said, "Does she have to be the one? Can't I do it, or somebody else?"

"Next of kin. But it doesn't have to be now. Morning's soon enough."

"Now," she said, "right now."

He said, "Lynn, please —"

"No. Will you take me? If not, he will. Or I'll drive myself."

"I'll take you, if you're sure it's what you want —"

"What I *want* is for my husband to still be alive." She did that habitual twining thing with her long-fingered hands. She was so pale now she might have been exsanguinated; the skin across her cheeks was almost transparent, so that you could see the veins, the crawling muscles beneath the skin. "I'll get dressed and we'll go. It won't take me long."

"You are dressed —"

"I can't go like this. For God's sake, Drew."

She twisted away from him, walked stiffly out of sight. He stared after her for a few seconds before he faced me again. Anguish showed in his dark eyes; he spread his hands in a helpless gesture.

"She'll be all right," he said. To himself mostly, as if he were trying to convince himself that it was true. "It'll take time, that's all. Time."

I stayed silent.

All he could find to say to me was, "Thanks for what you did," in a distracted voice.

"For nothing," I said.

I found my own way out.

Four thirty, a hint of dawn in the dark restless sky, when I got home. I let myself in as quietly as I could. Kerry had left a couple of lights on for me; I went down the hall, eased open the bedroom door. The night-light in the bathroom let me see that she was asleep. But she'd always been a fairly light sleeper and I knew that if I went in there and got undressed and got into bed, she would wake up and ask questions that I didn't feel like answering right now. More importantly, she needed sleep and she wouldn't get any more if I woke her up. Neither of us would.

I stood watching her for a time. She'd kicked off the blanket and sheet and lay sprawled out on her back, breathing in soft little snores, her auburn hair fluffed out around her head and one arm flung over on my side of the bed. She looked very young in that pose and that light, like Emily does sleeping. Young and innocent and vulnerable.

I love you so damn much, I thought. You have to tell me what's wrong, babe, let me do something, anything to help fix it. If I ever lost you . . .

But I wasn't going to let myself go there. Not after what I'd been dealing with. I eased the door shut again and shut off the hall light and catfooted into the living room. It was early-morning cold in there, and I hadn't been able to get warm since that first long walk on the beach; I turned the heat up past seventy. Then I took off my shoes and lay down on the couch with my coat on and Kerry's afghan pulled up to my chin. I thought maybe I could sleep a little, or at least lapse into a doze, but I was wide awake and I stayed that way as daylight began to creep in around the drawn drapes.

I kept seeing James Troxell's dead face, stark and bloody in the beam of my flashlight. And the film of windblown sand over his staring eyes. And the shiny new .22 in his stiffened fingers.

Suicide. Such a waste, such a stupid senseless needless waste.

And after a while it was another dead face I was seeing, another stupid senseless needless waste I was thinking about. Eberhardt's. Eberhardt, and the way he'd died.

23

Jake Runyon

The call came in on his cell phone shortly before eleven. He was in the field on new agency business, a routine investigation on behalf of the plaintiff in a wrongful death lawsuit. But the timing was good; he'd just parked his Ford on Stanyan Street and was walking down toward Haight where the subject of his first interview owned a music store, so he was able to take the call on the move.

He recognized the woman's voice even before she identified herself. "I hope I'm not calling at a bad time," she said. Tentative and apologetic, the way she would approach most things in her life. "This is Arlene Burke. Sean Ostrow's sister?"

"Yes, Mrs. Burke."

"I'm sorry I didn't call Saturday night or yesterday. I wanted to, but . . . well, my husband" — stress on the word husband, as if it were a bad taste in her mouth — "he didn't want me to have anything more to do with you. He threw a fit about it. He said you threatened him. Did you?"

"No, I didn't."

"I didn't think so. I suppose it was the other way around."

"He was abusive, yes."

"He can be such a bastard," she said with sudden vehemence. "If I'd known what he was, I never would have married him."

Runyon said nothing. She didn't expect a response; she was just venting.

There was a staticky hiss on the line, as if she'd exhaled sharply into the receiver on her end. "Well. You don't want to hear about any of that," she said. "I called for two reasons."

"Yes?"

"I found a photograph of Sean you can have. It's not recent, but it's a good likeness. Do you still want to pick it up?"

"Later today, if that's all right."

"It'll have to be here at Macy's," she said. "That's where I'm calling from, I'm on my break. I work until six tonight, so any time before then."

"I should be able to get there midafternoon."

"The other thing I wanted to tell you, I —"

The rest of what she said was lost in the diesel roar of a passing Muni bus. Runyon turned into the doorway of a bookshop, put his back to the street and plugged his other ear with a fingertip. When the noise subsided he said, "Sorry, I couldn't hear you."

"It sounds like you're on a busy street."

"I am. What was it you said?"

"I remembered something. About Sean's new job in the city."

"Yes?"

"He never said exactly what the job is, so I don't know if this will help. But he did say it was part-time and seasonal."

"Seasonal?"

"That was the word he used. But it didn't matter, he said, because it was a dream job, another dream about to come true."

"Also his exact words?"

"Well, I think so. That's what I remember."

"Any idea what the 'other dream about to come true' was?"

"No. But it could be the someone he met, whoever she is."

"This was in late March?"

"That's right. The end of March."

"And he left for the city on April first."

"Early that morning. That was the day he was moving into his new apartment."

"And the day he was starting his new job?"

". . . No, actually. I think he said he'd have some time to get settled first."

Runyon thanked her and rang off. Call Tamara right away or get the interview over with first? The interview was immediate agency business, the appointment time firm; Sean Ostrow was personal business, still unconfirmed and speculative. He left the doorway and threaded his way to the music shop through the neocounterculture types that crowded Haight Street.

Tamara said, "Baseball?"

"Ostrow's a big Giants fan."

"So you think this new job of his has something to do with the Giants?"

"Adds up that way. Baseball is seasonal, it's part-time work for everybody but players and management. Perfect fit for a guy like Ostrow."

"With the team itself?"

"Maybe."

"He's a teamster, right? Some sort of driving job?"

"That's one possibility," Runyon said. "But my guess is, it's connected with the stadium."

"Could be any one of a couple dozen jobs then."

"He told his sister it was a dream job.

For him that'd be one where he's inside the stadium while games are being played, in a position to watch. Narrows it down. Usher, security officer, one of the roving vendors."

"Shouldn't be any trouble finding out that much, as long as he's using his own name."

"No reason for him not to be."

"But if he is working at SBC Park, you won't find him there this week or next. Giants are on the road."

"I know. Can you get his address from their personnel file?"

"Tricky," Tamara said. "If the team and the stadium were city-owned, no problem — I could probably get it through Parks and Recreation. But they're privately owned. Limited partnership called . . . San Francisco Baseball Associates, something like that."

"There's police presence at the games. Couldn't your contact at SFPD turn up Ostrow's address?"

"Longshot. Officers aren't supplied by SFPD, they're off-duty cops hired by the SFBA. I know that because of an insurance case we had a while back."

"What about the rest of the park security force? Private firm?"

"Uh-uh. SFBA has their own security task force."

"Must be some way to get that address."

"Direct appeal to SFBA, maybe. If that doesn't work, I'll get creative."

"Anything you can do."

"Yeah, man," she said. "You just leave it to me."

24

Kerry

She was five minutes early for her two o'clock appointment with Dr. Pappas. Not that she had any intention of arriving early. Usually the six-block walk from Bates and Carpenter to the 450 Sutter medical building took a leisurely twenty minutes. Today she seemed to have done it in a fast fifteen. Her body trying to convince her head that it was in good shape in spite of what was growing inside it? Hey, look, I'm not a bit tired, brisk walks don't bother me. Next year why don't we sign up for the Bay to Breakers marathon? Sure, great idea. If we're still here next year.

She checked in at the desk and then sat on one of the uncomfortable chairs in the nondescript waiting room and opened an old issue of *People* and leafed through it without seeing anything on the printed pages. She was at ease, though. Not tense at all. Funny thing was, she'd always been at ease in doctors' offices, hospitals. Most people, like the one other person in the waiting room, a tight-lipped woman in an expensive Donna Karan suit, were time-conscious and showed little fidgety signs of nervous tension, as if they were afraid of receiving bad news. Not Kerry Wade. Always optimistic, that was her. Even now, when she knew the news she was going to be given was bad, had known it the instant Dr. Pappas's nurse called to ask her to come in for an immediate consultation, she was more or less relaxed. As though, ho-hum, it was just another routine visit to her gynecologist.

Still optimistic, too? Not as much as she had been, or tried to be, before the nurse's call this morning, but hopeful nonetheless. It was not in her nature to be downbeat. She was no longer even particularly upset, or resigned. What she was, she supposed, was numb. She'd passed through most of the emotional stages in the past week — fear, anger, anxiety, everything except denial. That was one of many things Cybil had taught her growing up: accept facts, face your problems, and then deal with them.

So far she'd accepted this fact, faced this problem, but she wondered again if it had been the right choice to do it alone except for Cybil. Same conclusion: Yes, even though it hadn't been easy. She'd come close to telling Bill the truth on Friday night; would have if Jake Runyon hadn't called when he did. She was glad then and still glad that she hadn't. He was strong, tough, courageous, but he was also emotional and overly sensitive and inclined to pessimism. If she'd burdened him with this from the first, he'd have been a basket case by now, and coping with that on top of the rest would have turned her into one. It had been hard enough telling Cybil, coping with her reaction and with her own worst fears about Russ Dancer. Hard enough dealing with the long wait as it was. And if the biopsy results had turned out negative, anguishing Bill prematurely would have been an unnecessary cruelty.

Now . . .

She couldn't keep it from him any longer, of course. Or from Emily. Unfair to both of them if she tried even for a little while longer; unfair to herself. She would need their support to get through what lay ahead. She'd always believed that any sort of physical illness was affected, positively or negatively, by the person's mental attitude — and her optimism wasn't unshakable. It would require plenty of shoring up over the next few months. . . .

The door to the inner offices opened and

the heavyset young nurse put her head out. "Ms. Wade? Will you come in, please?"

The tight-lipped woman shifted position on her chair and aimed a frown in Kerry's direction. Waiting longer, so she believed it should be her turn. Kerry smiled at her, thinking: *You don't know how lucky you are, lady. I wish all I was facing here was a little inconvenience and a sore butt.* It wasn't much of a private joke, but it allowed her to hold the smile in place as she followed the nurse inside.

None of the usual routine today of being weighed and having her pulse rate and blood pressure taken; nor was she deposited in one of the examining rooms as per usual. Ushered straight into Dr. Pappas's private office, where the doctor stood waiting behind her desk. The nurse closed the door behind Kerry as soon as she stepped through.

Audra Pappas had been her gynecologist for more than fifteen years. Their relationship was strictly doctor-patient, pleasant enough but without any personal connection. That was fine with Kerry, now especially. No-nonsense, straightforward professionalism was what she wanted and needed in the present circumstances. So was the air of authoritative competence she projected. Competence and efficiency were the two words that best described Dr. Pappas. Midforties, tall, sandy-haired, brusque, with very little if any sense of humor — as if life and the practice of medicine were too important to her to be tempered with either levity or social niceties.

She seldom smiled, but she smiled now, a brief stretching of her closed lips, as she took Kerry's hand — a firm handshaker, Dr. Pappas — and invited her to sit down. Professional, that smile, meant to be reassuring. If Kerry hadn't known what was coming, the uncharacteristic smile would have told her.

Pappas sat behind her desk, folded her hands on top of a thick file folder. The Kerry Wade file, no doubt. Wherein the damning evidence lay. At length she said, "I imagine you know why I asked you to come in this afternoon."

"The biopsy results. Bad news."

"Well, the results are not what we hoped for. To begin with, the biopsy surgeon wasn't able to remove the entire mass."

"Large tumor, then."

"Substantial, yes."

"And not benign."

"No. Malignant, I'm afraid."

Despite the fact that she'd prepared herself for it, the confirmation still jolted her a little. Malignant. What a nasty little word that was, one of those words that exactly fits and conveys its meaning. A *malignant* word.

She cleared her throat before she trusted herself to speak in a normal voice. "Do you think we caught it early enough?"

"I hope we have."

"Meaning it's too soon to tell?"

"Yes."

"So. What's the next step?"

"You'll need to consult with a cancer surgeon. As soon as possible."

"Is there one you recommend?"

"Dr. Emil Janek at UC Med Center is one of the best. I'll make an appointment for you."

"All right. And then what? Further tests, surgery?"

"Both."

"What kind of surgery? Lumpectomy?"

"Dr. Janek will help you make that decision. It depends, first of all, on the grade and stage of the tumor and whether its borders seem fairly distinct or not. The more diffuse the cells, the more invasive the cancer and the more radical the necessary surgery."

"Full or partial mastectomy."

"Yes. Some women opt for that in any case."

"Better chance of survival?"

"Actually," Pappas said, "clinical studies have shown there's a small difference in the survival rate between a lumpectomy and either type of mastectomy. The reason some women make that choice is the need for a period of radiation therapy following a lumpectomy."

"How long a period?"

"A minimum of six weeks, five days a week. Longer, if necessary, to make certain all the cancerous cells in the breast have been destroyed."

She dreaded the thought of losing a breast, of the need for reconstructive surgery or worse, a prosthesis. It wouldn't matter to Bill, would have no effect on their relationship, but it would matter to *her;* it was *her* breast, a part of Kerry Wade that would be lost forever. But the prospect of six weeks of radiation was no more appealing. Fatigue, all the other side effects . . . God.

"There are a number of other factors involved in the decision as to what's best for you," Pappas was saying. "Your age. The general state of your health, which is very good. The fact that you're postmenopausal. Your family medical history."

"There's been no incidence of breast cancer in my family," Kerry said.

"Any other type of cancer?"

"I'm not sure."

"You'll need to find out."

"I know. How long before we know how invasive the cancer is and what type of surgery I should have?"

"I can't give you an exact time line. You'll have to discuss that with Dr. Janek."

"Can my decision wait as long as two weeks?"

"Possibly. Why do you need that much time?"

Simple enough to explain. I might need that much time, doctor, because it may take that long to get the results of the DNA test. I don't know who my biological father is, you see — I don't know if I'm the daughter of the man who raised me or the child of a drunken rapist. And if I am the child of a rapist, then that makes the situation all the worse because he's dead and I don't know anything about his background or any way to find out if there was a history of cancer in his family.

But she couldn't say any of that to Dr. Pappas. And probably not to Dr. Janek until she found out one way or another. Her secret until then, hers and Cybil's and Bill's.

She cleared her throat again. "It's a personal matter."

"Having to do with your husband?" Pappas asked bluntly.

"No. Lord, no. He'll be supportive no matter what."

"Have you told him yet?"

"Not yet. I wanted to know the biopsy results first."

"Don't delay. This isn't something that should be faced alone."

"I know," Kerry said, "and I won't put it off. I'll tell him tonight."

"Good. And Kerry" — one of the few times Pappas had used her given name — "remember that breast cancer is not the devastating disease it once was. It can be treated, it can be cured in most instances of early discovery. Be optimistic."

"I am, doctor. I am."

So why did she feel, all of a sudden, as if she was going to burst into tears?

25

Jack Logan looked as Monday-morning tired as I felt. Rough weekend for him, too, for whatever reason. Eye bags, deep lines bracketing his mouth and nose, a patch of gray shadow on one side of his jaw where he'd missed with his razor. When I noticed the shadow I rubbed a hand over my face, and sure enough, my fingers scraped over a stubbly patch of my own. Some pair we made. A couple of old horses still out running around the track when we should have been pastured or in our home stalls taking it easy. Whether that meant we were blooded stock or just stupid-stubborn plugs was anybody's guess.

He'd gotten my message, but he didn't know about James Troxell's suicide until I told him. The wheels grind slow at SFPD these days. I gave him a verbal rundown, then handed over the extra copy of the client report to Lynn Troxell that I'd brought with me.

When he finished reading it he pinched

his eyes between thumb and forefinger, sipped coffee, looked out his office window at the stream of cars on the Bay Bridge approach. There was no point in trying to read his expression. I'd played poker with the man often enough to know it couldn't be done.

"What gripes me most about suicides," he said finally, "is all the damage they leave behind. Damage and loose ends."

"Total self-involvement. They stop caring about anything but their own pain."

"Yeah. So you're convinced the reason Troxell blew himself away is this death obsession he had."

"That, and the fact that he couldn't go on facing his own cowardice."

"No direct involvement in the Dumont homicide."

"Just what he evidently witnessed."

"You sure about that?"

"As sure as I can be without corroborating evidence."

"You think we'll find some among his effects?"

"I wouldn't be surprised."

"In that place he rented on Potrero Hill, maybe?"

"Could be."

"Uh-huh. How'd you find out about him being a witness?"

"Does it matter, Jack?"

"Depends on how relevant it is."

"Not very."

"We're not going to find anything else among his effects, are we? Any surprises?"

"I doubt it."

Logan drank more coffee, looked out the window again. The back end of the Hall of Justice practically abuts the 101 freeway approach; you could hear the steady thrum of traffic noise through the closed windows.

Pretty soon he said, "You should've come in with this as soon as you found out. Troxell might still be alive if you had."

"I know it. What can I say, Jack? I screwed up."

"Well, you're not the only one. The wife, the lawyer."

"We all made the same mistake. It looked like he was going to come in voluntarily. We wanted to believe it, so we believed it."

"Suicides. Christ. You just can't figure what goes on inside their heads."

"Sometimes you can," I said, "if you make the right connections."

"Yeah, well, not this time."

"No, not this time."

"So all right," he said, "it's over and done with. End of story, if what you've told me is true. You sure there's nothing else I should know?"

I hesitated before I said, "Not about Troxell."

"The Dumont case?"

"Jake Runyon's working on an angle he dug up, mostly on his own time."

"Yeah? Why's he so interested?"

"He feels sorry for the victim's sister. So he's doing it pro bono. Dog with a bone, you know how it is."

"What's the angle?"

I told him about Sean Ostrow.

"Sounds pretty circumstantial to me," Logan said.

"So far," I agreed. "No hard evidence of any kind. If there was, Jake would've turned it over by now."

"I hope so. For both your sakes."

"You want me to have him come in anyway, talk to you or the inspectors who caught the case?"

Logan thought about that. "Not much point. But if he does turn up anything definite, you send him in on the run. Got it?"

"Got it."

"Okay. Go on, get out of here. I've got a meeting in ten minutes."

Bullet dodged. I didn't waste any time taking myself out of the line of fire.

I caught up with Charles Kayabalian at Civic Center, in the City Hall lobby. He was defending the plaintiff in a civil suit, the judge had just called noon recess, and Kayabalian was on his way to lunch. He had no problem with me joining him. I wasn't hungry, but you have to eat — had better eat when you've gotten little sleep the night before and a developing head cold from all the running around in that Ocean Beach chill. The last thing I needed right now was to wind up sick in bed.

Rough weekend for Kayabalian, too. He didn't look as poorly used as Logan or me, maybe because he was several years younger, but the signs were plain enough on his thin, walnut-brown face. And in the fact that his usually impeccable attire was on the rumpled side today, the knot in his paisley tie just a bit off-center. He yawned more than once on our way to the restaurant on Van Ness.

Once we were seated with our lunches in front of us I asked him when he'd last talked to Lynn Troxell. He said, "Just before eight o'clock, briefly. I called to see how she was bearing up."

"And?"

"She sounded calm enough under the circumstances."

"Casement still with her then?"

"Yes. He answered the phone."

"Was he going to stay with her?"

"Until Lynn's sister could get there from Marysville. Lynn asked her to come — she needs family at a time like this and they're fairly close. Or Casement did the asking, I don't know. He said he was going to notify Martin Hessen and anybody else that needed to be told. Better him than me, frankly."

"The sister was coming right away?"

"As soon as she could. She may be there by now."

We talked a little more while we finished our sandwiches. My ham and cheese was going to lie in my stomach all afternoon; I could feel it hardening up in there already as we got up from the table. On the way out of the restaurant Kayabalian allowed that he would probably go over and see Lynn Troxell in person later today. "I'm not relishing the visit," he said. "A stranger's grief is bad enough, but in a friend or loved one . . . well, you know what I mean."

"All too well."

"You won't be seeing her again, will you?"

"Not right away, no."

But eventually. Like it or not, sooner or later — I was pretty sure of that.

★ ★ ★

At the agency, we had Sassy Tamara to start the week. Hip, flip, and cynical. I liked that version a lot better than Gloomy or Grumpy. At least she was more or less responsive.

When I asked her about her weekend, she said, "I almost got laid by a dude wanted me to wear Marilyn Monroe's hair."

"Huh?"

"Carries it around in his briefcase in case he gets lucky."

". . . Is that some kind of joke?"

"Yeah," she said. "On me."

Young people nowadays. Sometimes they seem to speak a language that sounds like English but makes no more sense to people of my generation than Urdu or Sanskrit.

We talked some, comprehensibly, about Troxell's suicide and Jake Runyon's unofficial investigation into the rape-murder of Erin Dumont, his call this morning with the baseball hunch. Tamara hadn't been able to track down a current address for Sean Ostrow yet, but she would. There was damn little information she couldn't dig up sooner or later; it was a matter of professional pride with her, in spite of all that office-drudge nonsense she'd given me.

283

"Sounds like Jake is convinced Ostrow is the perp," I said.

"Leaning heavy that way," she agreed. "Once he knows where to find Ostrow, he's gonna want to get in the man's face. You think we should let him go ahead? Or tell him to back off?"

"He's got good instincts. My inclination is to let him stay with it."

"We're off the hook now. Might put us right back on."

"I know it."

"But sometimes you have to keep pushing, right?"

"Sometimes your conscience won't let you do anything else."

"Just don't push too hard."

"That's the tricky part," I said. "Knowing how hard to push and when to stop before it becomes a shove."

I went into my office and put in a call to the Troxell home. Answering machine. I identified myself, but if anybody was monitoring calls, they didn't pick up. I left an "if there's anything I can do" message and let it go at that for now.

For a time I tried to do some routine work, but my head wasn't into it. Shortly before three o'clock I packed it in and went to tell Tamara that I was through for the day.

"Going home?" she asked.

"Not right away. Couple of things I need to do first."

"Business?"

"Pushing," I said.

26

Jake Runyon

Midafternoon traffic in Marin and Sonoma counties was heavy enough to cause slow-downs. The temperature was fifteen degrees warmer up there, summer-hot in the vicinity of Santa Rosa. The Ford's air-conditioning was busted, so Runyon drove with the window down. Windless heat mixed with exhaust fumes crawled through the car, sweating him and making him aware of how tired he felt. Lack of sleep seldom bothered him; all he'd ever needed was four or five hours a night. He remembered one hot summer in Seattle, when he was working vice. A string of violent assaults on prostitutes had everybody on the squad pulling extra duty, and he'd gone sixty-seven hours straight without closing his eyes and been as alert and functional when they finally cornered the perp in an abandoned building as if he'd just gotten out of bed.

Stop and go, stop and go. He kept trying to shut himself down in order to make the drive easier, but he was having trouble doing it today. The missed sleep, maybe. Memories kept intruding unbidden, like feelers probing through his mind and then expanding into sharp images.

That same summer he'd gone the sixty-seven hours without sleep. A few weeks later, early August, the much-needed vacation. Colleen had talked him into driving up to the Cascades, going camping in the national forest. He was an urbanite, he didn't know anything about wilderness camping, but he'd done it to please Colleen. And the experience hadn't been bad at all. All those giant trees, all that empty virgin quiet — peaceful and stimulating at the same time. Both of them enjoying themselves, frisking around in the woods like a couple of kids, Colleen playful and horny that one warm afternoon in the little meadow where they stopped to make camp. So there they were, going at it in the grass under towering redwoods, her on top and making more noise than she usually did, and then all of a sudden she'd let out a shriek that had nothing to do with their lovemaking and froze, pointed, and yelled, "Jake, look!" And he'd twisted around and looked, and damn if a bear hadn't been standing at the edge of the glade, watching them.

Small brown bear, but it looked big as hell

from down on the ground. They'd shoved apart and he'd jumped for his .357 Magnum, but he didn't need it. The bear had already taken off running by the time he got it out of his pack. And there they stood, buck naked, him armed and loaded for bear, listening to a real bear crashing away through the woods. Then Colleen started to laugh. "We scared him more than he scared us," she said. "I'll bet that poor peeping bruin doesn't stop running for hours." Her words got him laughing and they couldn't stop. They must've laughed for ten minutes, hanging on to each other and whooping it up like a couple of crazy people.

Their private joke for years afterward. All he had to do was wink and say "Peeping bruin," and Colleen would break up. That fine, rich, bawdy laugh of hers . . . he'd loved that laugh, nothing made him feel better than hearing her laugh —

A horn blared behind him, snapped him out of it. Cars were moving up ahead and he was still sitting there dead stopped. Christ. He accelerated to rejoin the flow, rubbing off sweat with his free hand. Freeway noise poured in through the open window, but he could still hear Colleen's laughter echoing inside his head. Echoing and then fading. And gone.

He paid attention to the highway, only the highway the rest of the way into Santa Rosa. It was just four o'clock when he rolled into the parking garage behind the downtown Macy's.

Arlene Burke wasn't on the checkout desk or the floor in the housewares department. One of the other clerks said she was working in the stockroom and went to fetch her. She had the photograph in her hand when she came out. She gave Runyon a wan smile, said, "We can talk back there," and led him to a corner near the stockroom door. The whole time she held her body turned a quarter to the left, to keep the right side of her face out of his line of vision. But he'd already seen the bruise along the cheekbone that a heavy application of makeup hadn't quite covered. He didn't say anything about it. She had enough hurt in her life as it was.

The photograph was a five-by-seven candid color shot taken at some sort of small dinner party by someone without much camera skill. It was more or less in focus, but off-center so that Sean Ostrow's right arm was missing from the frame. The rest of him was there from the waist up. Over six feet tall and suety fat — three discernible chins, bulging belly that seemed to start under his collarbone and showed beneath the hem of a tentlike blue T-shirt. Sandy hair pulled back tight on his massive skull, part of the ponytail visible behind one shoulder. Irritated frown on the thick-lipped mouth, as if he hadn't wanted his picture taken. Pretty much the image Runyon had expected to see, but that wasn't why Ostrow seemed vaguely familiar.

"You said this is a good likeness of your brother, Mrs. Burke?"

"As he looked back then," she said. "That was taken, oh, it must be four years ago."

"He's changed since?"

"Lord, yes. I almost didn't recognize him when he moved down from Sacramento."

"Why is that?"

"I'd never seen him that thin before."

"Thin? You mean he'd lost weight?"

"You didn't know about that? I thought you did, or I'd've said something on Saturday."

His fault, dammit. He hadn't asked the right questions. "How much weight did he lose?"

"Sixty pounds by then."

"Did he tell you why?"

"He said he was sick and tired of being fat. I thought he looked good at about two-fifty, but he wasn't satisfied."

"Kept on losing?"

"Oh, yes. It was like he was obsessed with being thin. Or on a mission to change his life. He hardly ate anything, twelve hundred calories a day, never any more. He always hated exercise before, but he'd started jogging and joined a gym and worked out regularly. He kept on the same program while he was here."

"How much weight had he lost the last time you saw him?"

"Close to a hundred pounds. Isn't that amazing? No more ponytail, either — his hair cut short and styled real nice. He looked wonderful, like one of the people on that TV show, *Extreme Makeover*. A new man, you know? I was so proud of him."

A hundred pounds. A new man. Runyon looked at the photograph again, worked on it with his imagination until he had a clear image of the man as he must look now — leaned down, the sandy hair cut short and restyled. Then he knew why the image was familiar.

The young guy Risa Niland had been talking to in front of her apartment building Saturday afternoon was Sean Ostrow.

On his way to the parking garage, he called the Get Fit Health Club. Risa wasn't there; the man who answered said she'd left

291

early, around four o'clock, he didn't know why. Runyon tried her home number. She wasn't there either; her machine picked up. He left a terse message asking her to call him as soon as she got in.

Sean Ostrow was the perp, all right. No doubt about it now. Obsessed with being thin, on a mission to change his life — that was why he'd quit SunGold and left San Francisco two years ago. Starting over, making himself into a new man. Motivated by an even greater obsession: Erin Dumont. Took two years before he was satisfied with the change, and then he'd moved back to the city and presented the new Sean Ostrow to Erin Dumont. And she'd rejected him again. Two years, all the sacrifice — for nothing. Rage and hatred consumed love and worship, and that was why Erin Dumont had been slugged, strangled, and raped.

What wasn't clear was why now, two months later, he was hanging around Erin's sister. The way he and Risa had been on Saturday — not like strangers meeting for the first time. How long had she known him? What was their relationship? What was brewing inside his head this time?

Runyon got the car out of the garage and onto the freeway headed south before he called the agency. He told Tamara about Ostrow's weight loss, and the fact that Ostrow had made contact with Risa Niland. She didn't waste any time with questions or speculations; she said, "You were right about him — he's the perp," and let it go at that. "Right about the Giants baseball angle, too. I talked to the vice president of guest services, man does the hiring at S.F. Baseball Associates. Ostrow was an usher at SBC Park."

"Was?"

"Hired in late March, fired in mid-April."

"Why was he fired?"

"He only worked one game, opening day. Called in sick the second day, didn't show up or call in the next two games."

"Mid-April," Runyon said. "Just a couple of weeks after the murder."

"Too sick over what he did to care about his dream job anymore."

"Fits along with the rest of it. You get his new address?"

"Not yet. Against SFBA policy to give out personal information."

"Yeah."

"But I think I've got a line on it. Felicia at SFPD. That's why I didn't call you. Waiting for her to get back to me."

"Today?"

"She said maybe. Let you know as soon as I hear from her."

Tamara called back forty minutes later, as he was climbing Waldo Grade to the tunnel above the bridge. "Got it," she said. "Eleven ninety-seven Twenty-seventh Avenue."

That was only a few blocks from where Risa lived, where Erin had lived. Ostrow had found a place as close to his obsession as he could get.

"Okay. Thanks, Tamara."

"What're you planning to do?"

"Find Risa Niland and warn her. Talk to Ostrow as soon as I can find him."

"Jake . . . go easy. You know what I'm saying?"

"I won't cross any lines if I can help it."

27

Risa Niland

He was waiting for her when she got home.

Street parking in the neighborhood was always a problem, after four p.m. especially. Tonight she had to drive around for ten minutes until she found a space, way over on Balboa, and walk back uphill lugging the three heavy plastic grocery sacks. She was beginning to hate this city. So wonderful when she first moved here all dewy-eyed from Green Bay — magical, as she'd said to Jake Runyon. Now, after seven years, the allure had worn off; now it seemed dirty, chaotic, inconvenient, cold, dangerous, ugly. And yet, as often as she'd vowed to leave if and when Erin's murderer was caught, move back to Green Bay or Milwaukee, start a new life there, she wondered if she could actually go through with it. Despite what had happened to Erin, despite the ugliness and the hatred she was feeling, San Francisco was home, California was home. Her job was here, most of her friends were here, Jerry was here . . . no, the hell with

Jerry, he didn't fit into the equation anymore. Did he? Oh, God, she didn't know what she wanted anymore. Yes, she did — she wanted things back the way they were, Erin alive, the good times with Jerry, life to be uncomplicated again. She wanted to be naïve and carefree, to live in a never-never land of magic and make-believe.

She sighed heavily as she reached her building. Another bad day, compounded by a mild hangover, and another bad night coming up. In the foyer she set the sacks down, fumbled in her purse for her key.

"Risa."

The voice came from just behind her, and when she turned, there he was. Hunched inside a tan parka, his sandy hair windblown, his big hands clenched in front of him in a funny way that made it seem, in that first glance, as if he was about to start praying.

"Oh, Dave, hi. What're you doing here?"

"Can I talk to you? I really need to talk."

There was something in his tone that made her look closely at him. What she saw shocked her a little. There was so much anguish in his cold-reddened face, in his pale blue eyes, it was like he was wearing some sort of tragedy mask. He'd been sad and hurting ever since she'd known him, Saturday even more so than usual, but to-night . . . he seemed almost ravaged.

"Risa? Just for a few minutes?"

"Are you all right? Has something happened?"

"No, I just . . . I can't keep it inside me anymore."

"Can't keep what inside you?"

"What happened, what I did. It's tearing me up."

"The accident, you mean? Your girl?"

"Yes . . . my girl. Please, Risa."

Compassion rose in her. She knew that ravaged look all too well; she'd seen it often enough in her own reflection after Jerry, after Erin. She didn't really want to talk to anyone tonight, least of all someone who was hurting as much as she was, but she couldn't bring herself to deny him.

"All right," she said, "for a few minutes. Help me with the groceries?"

He nodded, picked up the sacks while she keyed the front door. They had to wait for the elevator; somebody was coming down. Anna Cheung and her big chocolate lab, Arnold, on the way out for their after-work walk.

Anna said hello to her and then glanced curiously at Dave. He was watching Arnold. The dog was a crotch-sniffer; it tried to stick its snout between Risa's legs. She fended it off gently and immediately it tried to do the same to him. He backed away as if he were afraid it might attack him.

Anna jerked the leash. "Arnold, no. Sorry about that," she said to Dave. "I've tried everything to break him of that habit."

He stepped into the elevator without answering.

On the way up he said, "I don't like dogs. People shouldn't have them in apartment buildings."

"You'd never know Arnold lived here," Risa said. "He never barks. Crotch-sniffing is his only bad habit."

"Still a dirty animal."

Inside the apartment she started toward the kitchen, but he stopped in the living room and stood looking around. Stared hard at something, then, and she saw that it was the framed photograph of Erin on the mantel over the gas-log fireplace.

"My sister," she said. "Erin."

He put the grocery sacks down on the coffee table, went to the fireplace for a closer look. "She was beautiful."

"Yes. Yes, she was."

"So beautiful."

There was an odd inflection in his voice. He seemed . . . different, somehow, now that they were up here. A little strange. She wondered if she hadn't been too hasty in inviting him. She didn't really know him, after all, or anything about him. Well, it was too late now. Make the best of it and ease him on his way.

"I'll put the groceries away," she said. "Would you like something to drink?"

"What?"

"Something to drink?"

"No. I don't want . . . no."

She carried the sacks into the kitchen, put the milk and a couple of other perishables into the fridge. The red numeral 2 was blinking on the answering machine — two messages. Listen to them now or wait until Dave was gone? Might as well wait, they wouldn't be important anyway. She sighed and went back into the living room.

He wasn't there.

She blinked, surprised. Where? The bathroom without asking?

Small sounds reached her, and the surprise gave way to stirrings of alarm. Not the bathroom — one of the bedrooms. She hurried down the hall. She kept the door to Erin's room shut, but now it was open. That was where he was, inside, standing next to the bed with his back to the doorway.

"What're you doing in here?"

He turned, and what she saw then made the skin crawl across her neck and shoulders. He'd taken Mr. Floppy off the dresser, was clutching the stuffed dog against his chest with both hands. And crying. Silent tears, big and wet, rolling down both cheeks, his mouth drawn into a grimace of agony.

"Hers," he said. "Hers."

"Put it down. What's the matter with you?"

His shoulders trembled; more tears flowed. "I'm sorry. Jesus, I'm sorry. Please forgive me."

"For what?"

"I can't stand it anymore, I can't keep it inside. I wanted to tell you every time I saw you, but I couldn't, I couldn't until now."

"Dave, you're not making sense —"

"Sean," he said.

"What?"

"Sean, not Dave, Dave's my middle name. Didn't she tell you about me? Sean? I told her my name, I know I did. Didn't she say it even once?"

Understanding came in a single sharp burst, like something breaking open inside her. She was cold, hot, sick, furious all at once. "Oh my God!"

"I loved her," he said.

"You did it! You're the one! You killed Erin!"

"I loved her, I never meant to hurt her, you have to believe that —"

She flung herself at him, clawing with her nails, kicking at his shins. He dropped the stuffed dog and tried to push her away, saying, "Stop it, stop it!" One of her kicks landed squarely. He yowled and grabbed her, twisted her around in his grasp, one arm wrapped across her collarbone. She dipped her chin and bit him, hard, on the wrist. He yowled again and let go of her, and she spun away from him, ran away from him into the hall, into the living room. He was right behind her, stumbling into the wall, calling her name.

Kitchen, a weapon, a knife —

The door buzzer sounded.

The sudden noise threw her off-stride, caused her to change direction. But the door was too far away; he caught her before she could get there and push the button to unlock the downstairs door. His arms were like a vise closing around her, mashing her breasts painfully as he yanked her back against his body. He whirled her off her feet, her legs flying outward. The scream building in her throat died in an explosive "Uff!" as he slammed her against something yielding, the back of the couch. She bounced down onto the cushions, the two of them still twined together and his crushing weight on top.

For a few seconds she couldn't breathe. Black spots and needles of light pinwheeled behind her eyes. Then some of the crushing weight lifted, she was able to suck in air in openmouthed gasps. Another scream formed in her throat. He clapped one hand over her mouth, the other tight against her windpipe.

Dimly she heard the door buzzer again.

"Don't scream," he said, panting, "don't fight me anymore. I don't want to hurt you. Please don't make me hurt you."

She stopped struggling.

After a few seconds his hand loosened across her mouth, slowly lifted. "I mean it, don't try to scream. I will hurt you if you do."

She didn't move, made no sound. His other hand was still a heavy pressure at her throat. The rattling wheeze of her breath and his filled her ears. Whoever had been ringing from downstairs had gone away.

"Listen to me, Risa, you have to understand. I didn't want to hurt your sister. I swear to God. I loved her. I loved her so much."

He was still crying; his face was smeared with wet. His eyes begged her. She flashed hate at him in return.

"But I wasn't worthy of her. I knew that. She was so beautiful and I was nothing, a nobody, a fat slob. That's why I went away. To make myself worthy, so she'd love me the way I loved her. Two years. I lost a hundred pounds, cut my hair, didn't go anywhere or do anything except work and save money for when we were together. It was hard but I did it. For her."

Fatso! Oh God, that's who he was . . . Fatso!

"Two years. I couldn't stand not seeing her, so I drove down sometimes and watched her to make sure she was all right. She never knew, I never let anybody know. All those guys she dated, they weren't important to her. She was waiting for the man who was worthy." He was making little hiccuping sounds now, as if he might start to hyperventilate. "Two years and I was ready, I got the kind of job I always wanted, a nice apartment for us, all the money we'd need for a while. I went to see her after she got off work. I didn't tell her who I was, I wanted to see if she'd recognize me. She didn't. I asked her out, I wasn't even shy about it, but she said no. She didn't want anything to do with me. The next night I went to see her again. In the park, while she was jogging. I got her to sit in the car with me and I told her then who I was and what I'd done for her. But she still didn't want anything to do with me. She said she was going to marry somebody else, she said even if she wasn't she could never be with me. She said . . . she said every time she looked at me she'd remember the way I used to be, how fat I was, like a big fat dog, and she laughed . . . she laughed at me . . . two years and everything I did for her and she was laughing at me . . ."

His hand was no longer at Risa's throat; now he held her pinned at the shoulders. His face loomed close enough for her to smell his breath, feel the heat of it. She'd never seen more suffering in any human being — and it made her hatred burn even hotter. She wanted nothing more in the world than to rip that face off his head, shred his suffering between her fingers until there was nothing left.

"I don't remember what happened after that," he said. "I swear to God, I don't remember. I —"

"You beat her! You strangled her! You raped her!"

"I don't remember. I don't, I don't, I must have been crazy —"

"You raped her after she was dead!"

"No! I didn't know she was dead, Jesus I didn't know, I don't remember, I woke up and she was naked and I . . . she . . . I couldn't have done that to her but she . . . I don't . . . Erin . . . I'm so sorry . . ."

"You son of a bitch!"

"I don't know what to do," he said. "I can't work, I can't eat, I can't sleep. I tried to give myself up to the police but I couldn't do it, I couldn't tell anybody but you. I had to be close to you because you were close to her. . . . Forgive me, Risa. Please. Please. Please . . ."

She couldn't stand to hear any more. His words hammered in her ears, inflamed her with such fury that she couldn't think. Bile rose into her mouth. "I'll never forgive you, never!"

"Risa . . ."

"I hope you rot in hell!" And she hurled globs of spittle and vomit straight into that ugly suffering face.

Mistake, oh God, she realized that as soon as she did it.

An animal sound ripped out of him. One hand and then the other clamped like an iron collar around her throat.

28

The address was a private home in Forest Hills, one of the city's older residential neighborhoods west of Twin Peaks. You couldn't tell much about it from the street. More modern than some of the homes in the neighborhood, a hillside split-level on a narrow lot, with an unobtrusive redwood and brick facade. A curving set of stone steps led down to it through a southwestern-style rock-and-cactus garden. If you stood off at a side angle, you could tell that there were broad decks on both levels that would command views of Mount Davidson and portions of downtown and the bay.

It was nearly five o'clock when I got there. I went down and rang the bell. Nobody opened the door. I climbed back up and checked the enclosed platform garage along one corner of the property at street level. But it was just a box with no doors or windows so I couldn't tell if it was empty or not.

I sat waiting in the car. Might be a long

wait, but now that I was here I was inclined to stay put at least a couple of hours and probably longer; I have more patience than usual when it comes to specific business. Get this done tonight if at all possible.

The wait lasted exactly forty-seven minutes. A car came too fast around a curve in the street behind me: black Ford Explorer, big as hell, just the kind of wheels I expected him to have. Brakes squealed; he swung sharp into the driveway. The door ground up and the SUV disappeared inside. When he came out, pausing to close the door with an inside button, I was waiting for him.

He squinted at me out of bleary eyes. "Hey," he said, "what're you doing here?"

"Talk to you for a few minutes?"

"Lynn's sister is staying with her, if that's what you —"

"Kayabalian told me."

"Poor kid. She's in a bad way right now, but she'll get through it."

"With your help?"

"Right. Anything I can do. So what's on your mind?"

"How about we talk inside. More private."

"Sure, sure. No problem."

Down the flagstone steps again. He let us in, led the way through a wide foyer past a staircase to the lower level, into a living room that took up the entire width of the main floor. Wine-colored drapes were partly open over a picture window and sliding glass doors to the deck.

Casement said, "Man, I'm beat," and scrubbed a hand over his heavy crust of beard. In the house's stillness it made an audible sound like sandpaper on wood. "I need a drink. Get you one?"

"No."

There was a well-stocked bar along one wall, trimmed in leather with matching stools in the same wine color. Behind it, he rattled a bottle against the rim of a crystal tumbler. I gave the room a quick scan. White brick fireplace on the side wall opposite the bar. Burgundy-colored leather furniture, the floor polished hardwood with burgundy and white throw rugs. Half a dozen paintings, all modernistic abstracts, all with the same colors in them.

Casement came out from behind the bar with a half-filled glass, Scotch or bourbon. He'd seen me looking around; he said, "Some decorating job, eh? My ex-wife. She had shitty taste in everything except me."

He laughed at his own wit, took a long pull of his drink. I stood there watching him.

"Ahh," he said, "that's better. How about we sit down, put our feet up?"

"You go ahead. I'll stand."

"Suit yourself." He flopped into a chair at an angle to the fireplace. I moved around in front of him. "What're we talking about?"

"Tell you a little story first," I said. "Then we'll talk."

"Story? What kind of story?"

"About a friend and partner I had once. His name was Eberhardt, a former cop like me. Good man, basically, but he made mistakes and he had more demons than most of us. When our partnership and friendship busted up, he opened his own detective agency. But he couldn't make a go of it. He started drinking heavily, made more mistakes and slid into a deep hole he couldn't get out of. Things got so bad for him he lost his will to live, decided to take the coward's way out. He sat in his car one night in an alley off Third Street and tried to make himself eat his gun. Only he didn't have the guts to do it on his own. He called the one person left in his life who cared about him, and she came down, and he begged her until she gave in. He pulled the trigger but it was her hand that helped him do it."

Casement's expression was blank; I might have been telling him about the weather. He said without meaning it, "That's too bad. But why tell me?"

"You could say," I went on, "that Eberhardt committed suicide. He wanted to die, it was his finger on the trigger, he just needed a little assist. But you could also say that the person who gave him that assist was guilty of murder. By law in this state, that's what assisted suicide is — a willful act of murder."

He was getting it now. His thick eyebrows drew together; he shifted position on the chair and slugged more whiskey. "That doesn't have anything to do with me."

"I think it does."

"Yeah? Well, spit it out then."

"Troxell also had help committing suicide. Your help, your assist."

"You're crazy, man! I wasn't anywhere near Ocean Beach last night."

"You didn't have to be. But your hand was on that gun just the same. And that makes you guilty of murder."

"Jim was my friend, for Chrissake. Why would I want him dead?"

"Because he was in the way."

"What's that supposed to mean?"

"You know what it means. You're in love with his wife."

"Bullshit."

"It's plain enough," I said. "The way you look at her, act around her. You love her and you want her and you knew the only way you could have her was if Troxell was dead."

Casement threw down the last of the whiskey, shoved onto his feet. I set myself, but he wasn't coming my way. He swung across to the bar to slop more liquor into his glass. Stayed there with it instead of returning to the chair, cocking a hip onto one of the leather stools, as if he wanted distance between us while he regrouped. I didn't let him have it. I walked over there, slow, and stood even closer than before, just a few paces separating us.

Up went his glass. When it came down again, he said, "Maybe I do love Lynn in my own way. I never made any secret that I care about her. That doesn't mean I wanted my best friend dead so I could move in on her."

"Doesn't it?"

"What put that goddamn crazy notion in your head, anyway?"

"Little slips you made, little things she and Kayabalian and Troxell himself told me. Bits and pieces that add up to the same conclusion."

"Wrong conclusion."

I grinned at him. Wolf grin, just the baring of teeth. "Here's the way I see it. Sometime

311

after Troxell witnessed what happened in the park, he came to you and told you about it. Or you dragged it out of him. Doesn't matter which. He couldn't make himself go to the police and he couldn't confide in his wife, he wasn't made that way. But he was full of guilt and starting to unravel and he needed to talk to somebody. Who else but you, his best buddy since high school."

"Blowing smoke, man, that's all you're doing."

"He confided his obsession with death and suicide, too. And not in an offhand way, like you made it seem — straight from the gut. He was serious about putting himself out of his misery, he'd been building to it even before the Erin Dumont trigger. But some men, men like Eberhardt, men like Troxell, just can't do it on their own, no matter how much they want to die. You saw that. Saw your opportunity, hatched your little scheme, and went to work on him."

"How am I supposed to've done that, smart guy?"

"Couldn't have been too hard. You knew how to manipulate him — you as much as told me so yourself, all that stuff about getting him to tutor you in school, arranging for him to lose his virginity. Strong, confident jock, weak and emotionally screwed-

312

up nerd. Not much of a contest at all. Re-inforce his low self-esteem, lead him to believe his situation is hopeless and he'd be doing it for his wife as much as for himself, shore up his resolve and courage, finally offer to help him do the job."

That must have been pretty close to the way it happened. Casement fidgeted again, slugged more whiskey — about as much reaction as I was going to get out of him.

"You went to work on her, too," I said. "Kept telling her how worried you were about her husband and his mental state. Suggested she hire detectives to follow him. You wanted her to know just how bad off he was."

Between his teeth: "Why would I hurt her like that if I'm so much in love with her?"

"To make her need you, lean on you. It was also a way to set Troxell up for the final push over the line. You must've been happy as hell with my report, the suggestions I made, the weekend grace period. After I left you talked her out of notifying the family doctor; Kayabalian told me that. You didn't want any medical interference that might keep Troxell from listening to anybody but you after the confrontation. You spent a long time alone with him Saturday after-noon and part of Sunday — working on his hopelessness and death obsession, maneuvering him into a state where he could blow himself away.

"Mrs. Troxell hid his car keys Saturday, in a place he'd never think to look. But Kayabalian told me you were with her when she did it. Troxell didn't find those keys on his own; he'd've had to tear the place apart and he didn't, he slipped out of the house almost immediately after he got out of bed. He got the keys from you. You took them from the hiding place and handed them over before you left that afternoon."

I watched Casement's face closely as I spoke. No expression except for tight lips and a faintly throbbing vein in one temple. No sign of guilt or remorse. Incapable of either emotion; I had him pegged that way. Cold bastard. Self-involved, borderline sociopath.

"Why would a man like Troxell use a gun on himself?" I said. "That bothered me almost from the first. Wouldn't be his choice if he were doing it on his own — the idea had to've been planted in his head, nurtured. 'A small caliber handgun is quick and painless, Jim, you do it somewhere outside the home, out on the beach, say, and there's not much mess for anybody to clean up.' When he says he doesn't think he can shoot himself, you keep telling him he can, and show him just how to do it, and eventually you've got him convinced. 'With help you can find the necessary courage to go through with it. And I have all the help I need now.' Troxell's words to me on the phone Saturday night. I thought he was talking about going to the police, but what he was really talking about was putting that bullet in his brain."

"Bullshit," Casement said again.

"Then there's the clincher," I said, "the weapon itself. Brand-new twenty-two-caliber automatic. Where did he get it?"

"How should I know? Bought it someplace."

"Where?"

"A gun shop, where else."

"That's what you said this morning. But you know and I know nobody can buy a handgun in this state without a valid permit. Troxell never applied for one. I checked."

"So what? So some sleazeball dealer sold it to him under the counter. Or he bought it on the street."

"There aren't that many sleazeball dealers who'd risk a stiff fine and a jail sentence on such a small illegal sale. How would a man like Troxell, an advocate of gun control, go about finding one in the first place? Same thing for a street buy — how would he know where to go and who to approach? No, he had to've gotten the piece from somebody he knew."

"Not me."

"Closed-off type like him, no close friends except you — it couldn't be anybody else. You sell sporting goods, you have easy access to target weapons like the twenty-two he used."

"You can't tie that pistol to me," Casement said. "No way."

"Pistol. Right. That's another thing you said this morning. I told you and Mrs. Troxell that he'd shot himself, she said why did he do it that way. And you said, 'A pistol . . . that's as quick as it gets.' "

"Gun, pistol, what's the difference?"

"Pistol refers to a semiautomatic handgun. You damn well know that in your business. But I didn't say what kind of weapon Troxell used. It could've been a revolver, or even a shotgun or rifle."

"I just assumed it was a pistol. You can't prove any different."

"No?"

"No. Can't prove a goddamn thing you've said."

"I could try."

"Go ahead. You won't find anything."

"The police might," I said.

316

"Take this crap of yours to the cops? You do, you'll be one sorry son of a bitch."

"Is that a threat?"

"Damn right it's a threat. Any hassle, and I'll sue you for slander and defamation. I'll take everything you've got."

"You'd have to prove malicious intent. The malice here is all on your side."

"I'm warning you. Back off."

"No. I may or may not talk to the police. I am going to talk to the widow."

Blood-rush darkened his face even more. He said savagely, "You stay the hell away from Lynn."

"She has to know what you did."

"She wouldn't believe you."

"It's the truth. She'll believe it eventually."

"Goddamn you, I won't let that happen!"

"You don't have a tenth of the influence with her you did with her husband. If you did, you wouldn't've had to help him die to get your hands on her."

He slammed the glass down on the bar top, lunged off the stool and up close to me. I set myself again, arms out away from my body, but all he did was get into my face. "Stay away from her," he said, spitting the words, spraying saliva.

"All for nothing, Casement. She'll hate

your guts, she won't have anything to do with you."

"She will, she's mine now! You're not gonna take her away from me, not now, not you or anybody else."

"We'll see about that."

He grabbed handfuls of my shirt and jacket, yanked me up on my toes. "I'll kill you, you hear me? I'll kill you!"

I drove the heel of my left hand up hard against the tendons in one wrist, at the same time chopping down with my right on the other wristbone. The force of the moves made him yell, broke his hold and exposed the upper part of his body. I gave him a hard shove, two-handed against his chest. He went staggering backward, would have gone down if he hadn't collided with the bar stool; he caught it and used it to steady himself. If he'd charged me then, we'd've been into it hot and heavy and the advantage would have been his. But he didn't. He hung there, breathing hard, his face congested, glaring hate and rage at me.

"I'm half your age, old man," he said thickly. "I could break you in half."

"You could try."

"Beat the shit out of you and claim you attacked me."

"You wouldn't get away with that either. I

go back a long way in this city — I was a cop before I went into private practice. Lies about me and my methods don't get believed."

He didn't say anything to that. Heavy silence for a few seconds, broken only by the ragged rhythm of his breathing. Then he scraped his beard crust again, straightened, pushed the stool away from him. In a choked voice he said, "Get out of here. Get the fuck out of my house."

"Gladly."

I moved away from him sideways, keeping him in sight, in case he had any ideas about mixing it up again. No ideas, but more vicious words as I reached the hallway. "I meant what I said. You take Lynn away from me, I'll kill you."

For an answer I showed him the wolf grin one more time.

Outside the wind chilled me, brought the realization that I was sweating. I took a couple of long breaths, calming down, as I climbed to the street. In the car I took the voice-activated recorder from my coat pocket and ran the tape back far enough to be sure it was all on there. The recorder, one of Tamara's recent purchases for the agency, was state-of-the-art; both our voices were clear and distinct. Okay. I hadn't been able to maneuver Casement into a direct admission of guilt, so I probably still didn't have enough to go to the law. Kayabalian could tell me when I played the tape for him.

One thing for sure: Casement had said more than enough to convince Lynn Troxell when she heard it.

29

Jake Runyon

When he pulled up in front of the multiunit apartment building on Twenty-seventh Avenue, he unlocked the glove compartment and slid his .357 Magnum from inside. He checked the action and the loads, fastened the holstered weapon to his belt above the right hip so the tail of his jacket would cover it. Then he went to ring the bell to Sean Ostrow's apartment.

No response.

Back in the car, he drove out Twenty-ninth Avenue to Risa Niland's block. He scanned the parked cars on both sides as he rolled along; none was familiar. The only free curb space on the block was too short for the Ford, but he jockeyed it in there anyway. The overhang into one of the driveways was enough to piss off the owner or tenant but not enough to block access.

No response to her bell either.

He didn't like that; she should be home by now. Unless she had a date, and if she did, what if it was with Ostrow? No easy way of finding out one way or another, nothing much he could do except wait it out. Maintain a revolving surveillance between here and Ostrow's building until one of them showed up.

On the sidewalk again, he paused and then went to the corner to eye-check the cars parked on the uphill and downhill sides of Anza Street. An older brown model midway up on this side caught his attention. Ford Taurus? He climbed to it. Taurus, all right. And the license number was 2UGK697.

He liked that a hell of a lot less.

When he got back to the corner, a young Chinese woman with a dog on a leash was just turning in under the canopy above the entrance to Risa's building. Runyon hurried after her. She was at the door, with her key out, when he came into the foyer. The dog heard him and made a friendly rumbling sound, and that brought her around. He wasn't anybody she knew and his sudden appearance put her, if not her animal, on guard. He saw her shift the keys in her hand, one of them protruding between the index and middle finger, the way women were taught in self-defense classes. Good for her.

She said warily, "Are you looking for someone?"

"Risa Niland."

"Oh. Well, she's home."

"I just rang her bell. No answer."

"No? I saw her a little while ago, in the lobby."

"How long ago?"

"I don't know, about half an hour. They must've gone out."

"They?"

"She was with somebody."

"Guy in his twenties, big, sandy hair?"

"That's right . . ."

Runyon said, keeping his voice calm, "Open the door, please, miss."

"What?"

He slid the license case out of his pocket, flipped it open and held it up long enough for her to verify his photo and identify the official state seal. If that didn't work, he'd have no choice but to show her the Magnum. "Open the door, please," he said again. "The man with Risa Niland may be the one who murdered her sister."

"My God! Are you serious?"

"Dead serious."

Hesitation, but only for a beat or two. She used her key and then stepped back quickly, pulling the dog with her.

He said, "Better lock yourself in your apartment," and went through into the lobby. He bypassed the elevator, took the stairs in a light-footed run. Near the third-floor landing he drew his weapon, held it down along his leg as he shouldered through into the short hallway. Empty. Three-A was the door on the left; he eased over to it, laid his ear against the panel.

They were in there, all right. Muffled voices, the words not quite distinguishable but sharp-toned and a few octaves above normal. He could almost feel the tension in them.

He tried the knob with his left hand. Locked. The door looked solid, the lock was a good-quality deadbolt. You wouldn't be able to force it; kick it in, maybe, but it would take more than one or two kicks. Shooting it open wasn't an option. That left only one way to go.

More sounds in there. Words, movement.

He shifted the Magnum to his left hand, pounded on the door with his right — fast and hard, rattling it in its frame.

Scrambling noises, some kind of brief struggle. And then a woman's voice, Risa's, crying for help.

Runyon shouted, "Open up! Police!"

Man's voice, exclaiming something. Another cry from Risa.

Then she screamed, a rising sound suddenly sliced off.

He felt the scream as much as heard it, as if it were something thin and hot that had pierced his flesh. He had to try to get in there. He stepped back for leverage, drove the bottom of his shoe against the panel next to the lock. No give, like kicking a wall. He yelled in frustration and kicked out again, same result, and in his half frenzy he made the mistake of trying it the other way, by lowering his shoulder and hurling his weight forward into the door. He hit it squarely, but the lock still held and the solid wood bounced him off.

At almost the same time there was a sharp snick of metal, the lock being thrown inside, and the door was suddenly yanked open. And for an instant he was looking into Sean Ostrow's wet, wild eyes.

He still had his balance, but his feet weren't braced and he had no time to set them. Ostrow came through the doorway in a blind rush, hit him full on and drove him backward into the hallway wall. The impact jarred him enough to loosen his grip on his weapon, nearly drop it. By the time he got his equilibrium back, Ostrow was pounding down the stairs.

The apartment door was wide open. Runyon shoved over there first, bent a look inside. Risa was down on one knee in front of a long couch, her head up and her eyes as wild as Ostrow's. A thin line of blood made a jagged lightning slash on one cheek. She saw him and flapped one hand in a shooing gesture, saying, "I'm all right, I'm all right, don't let him get away, he killed my sister!"

Runyon turned away immediately. He could still hear Ostrow on the stairs, the flight from the second floor to the lobby now. He shoved the Magnum into its holster and plunged down himself, vaulting over two and three risers at a time, using both hands on the railing to keep his balance. The lobby was empty by the time he reached it; so was the sidewalk out front under the canopy. He banged through the door, onto the sidewalk looking left, right, left again. No sign of Ostrow.

The Anza Street corner, the parked Ford. Runyon ran that way, slanted a look uphill. And there he was, staggering around to the driver's door of the Taurus.

"Ostrow!"

The shout twisted the sandy head around, froze him for a second in the street. Runyon didn't draw his piece, didn't even think about it; he had no legal right to run around waving a loaded weapon on a city street, and it was a damn good way to get yourself shot by a passing cop or a citizen playing Dirty

Harry besides. He yelled Ostrow's name again and went charging up there.

Ostrow had no time to get into the car, get it started, get away. His freeze lasted another second, and then he broke into a run himself, uphill in the street.

Thirty yards separated them when Ostrow reached the top of the hill. He threw a look over his shoulder, saw how close behind Runyon was, and put his head down and veered to his left across Thirtieth Avenue. Brakes screeched and a minivan rattled by, the driver's startled face framed in the side window, as Runyon reached the crest. Ostrow was running diagonally, up onto the opposite sidewalk toward where the street humped and fell away downhill. But he didn't go that far. He cut sideways onto a narrow stretch of unpaved ground between the sidewalk and the cyclone fence that enclosed Washington High School's athletic buildings and football field.

Ahead of him, the fence made a perpendicular jog from where it bordered the far edge of the unpaved ground, back along the edge of the sidewalk. The perpendicular section was maybe a dozen feet wide and lower than the rest of the fence, no more than six feet high, because of a tall cedar tree growing on the inside. Ostrow didn't slow down; he hit the six-foot section at full speed, clawed his way up over the top, dropped down in an awkward stagger, and plowed into the cedar's trunk when he tried to right himself. Exposed roots tripped him. He slid on his ass down a short grassy embankment out of sight.

Runyon didn't slow down, either. He hit the fence just as hard, tore up his hands on the sharp jutting wire ends at the top as he heaved his body up and over. The pain was like an adrenaline rush. He steadied himself against the tree trunk, looking for Ostrow. Spotted him running along the red composition rubber track that circled the football field. Runyon avoided the cedar roots, managed to keep his footing to the bottom of the incline.

Ostrow saw him coming and veered off the track onto the broad, empty field. But he was either tiring or losing the panic-stimulus for his flight, stumbling and lurching a little now each time he cast glances over his shoulder. Runyon was winded too but running on thick, newly mowed grass was easier than doing it on asphalt and he didn't slow, didn't waver. The gap between them closed to twenty yards. Fifteen. Ten.

Ostrow went down.

One more backward look, and all at once

his legs seemed to give out and he fell, sprawling on his side, rolled over, crab-crawled and then tried to stand up. But Runyon was right there, looming above him, the Magnum out now in case there was any fight in the man, the weapon close to his chest and his body shielding it from the street above.

No fight. Ostrow quit trying to get up and knelt there gasping, staring up at Runyon with sick-dog eyes. Damp grass clippings clung to one side of his face. A thin band of foamy drool dribbled from his mouth.

Runyon said, "Get up."

The sandy head wobbled sideways, maybe a refusal, maybe something else. The tortured gaze shifted to the Magnum.

"Please," he said.

Runyon was silent, working to bring his breathing under control.

"Shoot me," Ostrow said. "Why don't you?"

"No."

"I want you to. I killed her, I deserve to die."

"I'm nobody's executioner."

"Please, I'm sorry . . . I'm so sorry . . ."

"Don't tell me," Runyon said. "Tell the judge and jury. Tell God."

Ostrow flopped over on his belly, buried

his face in the grass. Broken sobs came out of him — for the woman he'd killed or for himself, there was no way to tell which.

Later, after Ostrow had been taken away in handcuffs and the last of the police had gone, he had a little time alone with Risa. She was tearfully grateful to him. Told him she always would be. Told him he'd given her the closure she needed to stop grieving, get on with her life. When he was ready to leave, she hugged him tightly and clung to him for a few seconds, her body pressed against his.

She wasn't Colleen, she was Risa. She didn't even look much like Colleen, really. And Colleen was gone and he was still alive and Risa was an attractive woman and not married anymore. He wanted to ask if he could see her again, maybe take her to dinner or a movie. But the words wouldn't come.

He stood rigidly in her embrace, not able to return it, not able to make himself say anything at all.

30

I stood on the condo's balcony, watching the night. One of those rare, crystalline early-summer nights, no clouds and mostly wind-less, where both the city lights and the stars have a kind of hard metallic glitter that almost hurts the eyes.

So many stars tonight. If it wasn't for the light pollution, you would have been able to see the Milky Way. I looked for the two Dippers, found the Big but not the Little. Kerry knew where they were, knew the names and locations of all the major stars and constellations — just one of many things she knew that I didn't. I could identify the two Dippers and Venus, the evening star, but that was about all. Star clusters were just that to me; I looked at them, tried to imagine horses, birds, dogs, lions, fish the way she did, and couldn't seem to form the right pictures. Orion, Ursa Major, Gemini, Cassiopeia were just names to me.

Cancer had been just a name until tonight.

Cancer, the crab. Perfect fit, all right. Ugly, scuttling, sharp-clawed creature that tore through flesh, fed voraciously on human cells.

I was having trouble imagining that, too — the crab wreaking its havoc inside Kerry. Bad enough, the scare I'd had years ago, the spot on my lung from years of heavy smoking. But that scare had been false. This one was real. The spot hadn't been malignant. The lump in Kerry's breast was. And the victim wasn't me, it was the one person I loved more than my own life. That made it harder to deal with, because back during my brush with the crab I hadn't had her, I'd had no one to care about but myself.

I wished again that she'd told me as soon as the lump was discovered. And again, perversely, hating myself a little, I was glad she hadn't. Now at least I could focus my fear, concentrate my hope — I was better equipped to handle what lay ahead for Kerry, and for Emily when we told her. She'd known that about me. She knew me so well, better than I could ever know myself.

One good thing: it would be the last of the secrets between us. We'd vowed that to each other inside, before I came out. No more secrets. It was a vow we'd both keep. How could we not keep it, now?

Behind me the sliding glass door whispered open, whispered closed. Kerry came over to stand next to me, close. She'd put on a sweater, was holding it wrapped around herself with her arms crossed.

"You okay?" she said.

"Yes." More or less. "I just needed some air."

"Chilly out here."

"Not too bad. Supposed to warm up tomorrow, stay nice for a while."

"I hope so. I always feel better when the sun shines."

"So do I."

Neither of us said anything more for a time. Feeling welled up in me, sudden, sharp, and I straightened from the railing and turned her and held her again, the way I had inside after she told me.

"I love you," I said.

"I know," she said. "I love you."

"We'll get through this. It'll be all right."

"I know that, too."

We kept holding each other, tight, tight, and I looked up once more at all those bright glittering anonymous stars.

Don't let her die, I thought. You hear me up there?

You better not let her die.

About the Author

Bill Pronzini has published more than sixty novels, including three in collaboration with his wife, novelist Marcia Muller, and thirty-one in his popular "Nameless Detective" series. His work has been translated into eighteen languages and published in nearly thirty countries. Pronzini has received three Shamus Awards (two for Best Novel), the Lifetime Achievement Award from the Private Eye Writers of America, and six nominations for the Mystery Writers of America's Edgar Allan Poe Award. His novel *Snowbound* was the recipient of the Grand Prix de la Littérature Policière as the best crime novel published in France in 1988. *A Wasteland of Strangers* was nominated for the best crime novel of 1997 by both the Mystery Writers of America and the International Crime Writers Association. A young-adult short story, "Christmas Gifts," was the recipient of the Paul A. Witty Award presented by the International Reading Association for the best short fiction of 1999. He lives in northern California.

We hope you have enjoyed this Large Print book. Other Thorndike, Wheeler or Chivers Press Large Print books are available at your library or directly from the publishers.

For more information about current and upcoming titles, please call or write, without obligation, to:

Publisher
Thorndike Press
295 Kennedy Memorial Drive
Waterville, ME 04901
Tel. (800) 223-1244

Or visit our Web site at:
www.gale.com/thorndike
www.gale.com/wheeler

OR

Chivers Large Print
published by BBC Audiobooks Ltd
St James House, The Square
Lower Bristol Road
Bath BA2 3BH
England
Tel. +44(0) 800 136919
email: bbcaudiobooks@bbc.co.uk
www.bbcaudiobooks.co.uk

All our Large Print titles are designed for easy reading, and all our books are made to last.